Legacy

D1527366

Melissa Goetz McCaughan

Copyright © 2015 Melissa Goetz McCaughan

ISBN:1511747633
ISBN-13:978-1511747639

In memory of my grandmother, Romagene Brown
Her invincible spirit and legacy lives on.

ACKNOWLEDGMENTS

Thank you to early readers Nicole Emery, Tricia McKenny, Christine Meyers and Tiffany Boone for your valuable feedback and support.

Thank you to Michael Ireland for the cover design and Tracie Ross for the publicity photos.

To my mother, Reva Bell, thank you for reading to me as a child and instilling my love of the written word.

Thanks to my husband, Michael for believing in me and my son, Nicholas, who will always be my greatest creation.

"Not until we are lost do we begin to understand ourselves"
~Henry David Thoreau

1

Anna watched as the light beams danced from one leaf to the next as she drove under the ornate archway inside the cemetery gates. She knew the way intuitively. Yes, she had been to graveyards before, but this was her sanctuary. A right, then another right, then another right--this was the path to her past, and she hoped to a future that would illuminate the shadows in her mind.

Anna parked. She walked along the gravel road back to the private gravesite, her family's ancestral plot. Blocked by a sawhorse, it was one of the few spots in the graveyard where cars weren't allowed to drive up by the graves. The sky was fading to gray and Anna wondered if she should turn back. She pulled her travel umbrella out of her pocket, hoping her notebook wouldn't get wet, as she planned to stay until it got dark. She brought her rain jacket in case it started to pour, and a snack of raisins and chocolate – can't leave home without chocolate.

This cemetery, Pine Grove, was where Anna liked to do her writing – quiet, peaceful, no sounds except the distant hum of traffic along the interstate. Somehow her thoughts flowed more freely here – the dead quieted her inner critic. Images flashed across her mind, thoughts flowed like a solemn cavalcade of hearses at a funeral, mindful and not in a rush – if she ever was to write a novel, this was the place it would come to her.

But where was she to begin? She walked along the neatly trimmed grass, gazing at each headstone as she passed by, straining to read the older inscriptions. Her fingers grazed the marble etchings, hoping the worn hieroglyphics would be legible by some instantaneous ability of hers to read Braille. She stopped to pick a dandelion and twirled it between her fingers.

So bright and cheery dandelions are – until little children come along and pluck their heads off, she thought.

She lately felt a lot like a plucked dandelion. Anna didn't know whether she was coming or going. But, today she felt she was tired of the negativity of the world. Anna just wanted to retreat to her graveyard refuge and write – write until the pain subsided into a dull ache.

She hadn't always been so depressed. It seemed to increase with each passing year and disappointment. She used to be an idealist, inspired to "climb every mountain and chase every dream." You would have thought Julie Andrews and Anna were separated at birth. As a child, she was the one to lead all of her friends on imaginary adventures through dense forests into foreign lands filled with castles, dragons to slay and princesses to be won. Whenever a rainbow came out, she exclaimed "Look, follow it to the pot of gold!" and went running down the hill in her parents' backyard. But, cynicism set in when she was faced with the realities of life.

How many pots of gold had she actually found in her three decades upon this planet? Not too many. She pledged to write a novel since the age of eight. She came here weekly to her sanctuary since age 20 in hopes of catching a moment of inspiration. But, every Sunday, she left with nothing but scribbled thoughts on a ragged notebook page – not one full page had she ever written.

Some writer.

Anna walked over to the most prominent landmark of her ancestral plot – the monument erected by Jacob Hoffner. The monument was built to resemble a church. A tall ornate steeple protruded from the center with four smaller steeples shooting up from each corner. Four carved-out oval doorways allowed a glimpse of the solitary female statue inside.

She must have been a beautiful statue at one time – dressed in a toga with her curled hair pulled back and crowned with a wreath of roses. A basket of roses sat near her bare feet, a pile of roses were gathered in her skirt, rose petals lay scattered all around. She was innocent, demure in her long flowing gown, but at the same time, carved into a sensual figure that spoke of a great love. Sadly, she had become weathered with time, causing black soot to appear in her hair and along the right side of her face. Her eyes were encircled in a smoky outline that made them seem more painted than statuesque. The stark contrast of black and white gave the appearance of innocence worn away by old age. Her nose was broken off, as well as her forearms, and yet she stood, majestic overlooking the cemetery grounds as if they were her own.

At the base of the statue was an open marble book with an inscription that read, "This monument was erected June 23, 1882 by Jacob Hoffner to the memory of his wife Elizabeth and their children, Thomas, Jane, Jacob and James."

How sad to have seen your whole family die before you, she thought.

Anna walked around the monument to the stairs where she always sat and thought about writing. There were 28 irregularly placed stairs leading down to a platform that overlooked the grounds. The stairs were worn with large cracks in them, ivy pushing up from beneath.

What an ingenious idea to give visitors to your grave – somewhere to walk and contemplate your timely demise, she thought.

Jacob lived 95 years – that must have been unheard of in the 1800s. He was privy to all the great events of that century – the Civil War, the beginning of women's rights, and all the great writers who lived then - Wordsworth, the Brontes, Dickens, Thoreau.

Oh, to read those authors while they were still alive – how amazing that must have been.

At the base of the stairs sat the lions, one on each side. They guarded his grave as though someone might steal him. They were large, granite beasts and yet, they looked almost friendly. They faced outward toward the overlook as if he intended for them to enjoy the view. The one lion had his paws crossed and his head lying sleepily on his paws as if he was just settling in for a siesta. The other looked out with his mouth slightly open, as if he was watching something interesting down the hill. Sometimes she would pet them as if they were her friends. Friends were in short supply these days.

The sky was starting to darken. Anna hoped it wasn't going to rain too hard. No matter, she had stayed here for hours in the rain before – it just made it more difficult to write without soaking her notebook. She bunched her rain jacket around herself to fight off the chill. She walked down a couple more steps and sat on the level platform.

Anna got out her notebook and her lucky green pen and stared at the blank page.

What do I have to write about?

The pursuit of success? She certainly didn't have that in the material sense. She worked a mind numbing temp job at the FedEx warehouse. Her mother begged her to go back to college. Her professor had praised her creativity and often read her stories aloud in class. But, she had neither the self-confidence nor the self-discipline to stick with it. If only she had believed in herself. But, she had too many people call her dreams impractical and foolish. So, she quit college and applied at a temp agency for the first job available. She followed the rules and did as she was told, but it ate her up inside.

All of her life she had listened to other people tell her who to be – parents, teachers, society, the media, bosses, lovers and friends. Anna was such a quintessential people pleaser that the din of their voices rang in her ears even when no one was speaking. She couldn't hear her own voice or any kind of inner muse. It was choked and drowned out by the voices around her. So, she checked out, lost herself in TV, mindlessly surfed the computer, stopped seeing her friends – and came to the graveyard to be alone.

She listened to the stillness, to the hum of the traffic, to the leaves rustling in the trees. She longed to hear her own thoughts, unfettered by the demands and expectations of other people. Twelve years of therapy was unable to do what the silence could do – provide a sense of relief.

The breeze. . . there was always a breeze up there, no matter what the weather. Her long blonde hair flew in the wind and lightly fell upon her face, tickling her nose. Church bells played in the distance, reminiscent of some old steamboat calliope. That was one reason she liked to come on Sundays. The church bells were hypnotizing. Her eyes started to grow heavy. Sometimes being here went beyond providing a sense of peace to lulling her to sleep. She yawned.

Maybe she should write about love? She had been with her boyfriend, Patrick for almost two years. When she first met him, she was swept away by his charm and good looks. He was an actor. She saw him in a show, and met him at a coffee shop later that night. She was star struck. But, as the months passed and the attraction cooled, she wasn't sure what they really had in common. They seemed to be at a crossroads, two people wanting completely different things in life. And yet, she stayed hoping things would change. She spent years bouncing from one short-term relationship to the next. She was tired of starting over. She wanted to settle down with someone and be happy. She just wasn't sure if Patrick was "the one."

She scratched out the word "love." A story about that simply wasn't to be. Anna started to doodle and chew on her pen. It was starting to sprinkle. She scratched at the ketchup stain on her jeans. She lay back on the stairs and stared at the lush, green grass.

I wonder who would visit me if I died? she pondered.

She couldn't think of too many people. She didn't think anyone would remember her after she was gone.

If she could only write a book, that would be something. Someone could find it in a used bookstore one day and know some inner part of her soul that no one living could understand.

But, what to write?

She got out a chocolate Easter bunny and raisins. Perhaps food would clear her thought processes. She bit the bunny's ears off and wadded up the colored foil. Delicious. . . but not necessarily activating the brain waves. Maybe meditation would help. She crossed her legs in yoga-like fashion, touching her thumbs and forefingers together and resting them on her knees. She breathed in deeply and exhaled.

In..one..two..three..four.

Out..one..two..three..four.

Make your mind a blank and see what comes, she thought to herself.

Anna relaxed her shoulders. Her breathing deepened. Thoughts of the last few days flashed in front of her eyes – breakfast with Patrick this morning, moving boxes at her temp job at the factory, arguing with her sister over holiday arrangements.

Relax.

Her eyes grew heavier and heavier. She lay down on the stairs for a moment. Her eyes flickered and she saw the storm clouds moving swiftly off to the east. Her eyes closed again and she lost consciousness. The hum of the traffic faded away. Peace at last.

2

J acob had not slept for days. His eyes were red with exhaustion. He worried he would not make enough income to sustain the family through the winter. He had been home for weeks on bereavement leave and was behind on his work. Jacob thought he would leave for a few hours to consult with his business partner, Matthew, if Elizabeth could be left alone. She had been fragile these last few weeks and he was afraid to leave her by herself.

I am so lucky to have been blessed with such a beautiful wife, Jacob thought.

The first time he saw her was at the county fair. She was dressed in light blue and ivory. Her long chestnut hair was tied up in a bun with tiny curls framing her face. He asked her if he could buy her a soda.

"Only if you buy me some taffy, too" she said with a smile.

He was hooked from the moment he saw her. As they grew closer, he was touched by her gentle kindness with others and how patient she was with his little eccentricities.

Jacob walked into the bedroom.

"Elizabeth, it's time to wake up, darling."

Jacob always woke up long before dawn to care for the animals and do some writing and let Elizabeth sleep in.

"But, I'm so tired," yawned Elizabeth rolling over.

"Come on darling, you're going away tomorrow."

Elizabeth had been in a deep depression since their only child had passed away from fever. Baby Thomas was the only one to survive after a series of stillbirths. She loved so fiercely that she could not let the child go, could not erase the sound of his cries from her mind.

My poor, dear Elizabeth, Jacob thought.

At times, he worried that she might not make it. He feared that their grief would tear them apart. But, Elizabeth slowly found the courage to keep breathing these past six weeks. On occasion, the tired look in her eyes would sparkle ever so slightly. It gave Jacob hope.

Jacob walked downstairs, lit the lamps and put a kettle of water on the stove.

He called up, "Elizabeth, darling, you really must get up. You have a lot of packing to do."

Jacob heard his wife stir and heard the floorboards creaking overhead. He busied himself about the kitchen, pulling out a loaf of bread and a jar of honey for a small breakfast. He wasn't skilled in the kitchen, but he did what he could to make things easier for Elizabeth since the loss. After a few minutes, he saw her at the top of the stairs, her hair pinned up in a bun, wearing a simple, pink dress and looking sad but ethereal. She descended the staircase and took a seat at the oak table as her husband fussed about her with tea and toast.

"I thought we might take a walk about the gardens this morning," Jacob suggested.

"That would be nice," Elizabeth agreed with a slight smile on her lips.

He brushed a tendril of his wife's hair away from her eyes.

"I'll miss you while you're gone," he said.

"Then maybe I shouldn't go, Jacob. Miriam probably

wouldn't enjoy my company anyway," she said.

"Nonsense. She'll be delighted to see you and it would do you some good to get out of the house and see people," said Jacob.

They finished their breakfast and Jacob took his wife's hand and led her out back to their gardens. Jacob was something of a collector. He had traveled to Europe four times and marveled at the sculptures and gardens. He especially liked the stone animals – eagles, lions, swans. Their marble beauty seemed to him to be majestic and strong. Elizabeth and Jacob walked along the cobblestone path and marveled at the blue jays in the fountain, the daffodils springing up near the pond, and the frogs leaping from lily pad to lily pad.

"I must sit down a minute, darling," Elizabeth said.

They found a stone bench and took their rest. She shivered in the cool morning air.

"Are you going in to work, today?" Elizabeth asked.

"Just for a few hours," said Jacob. "I'll be home to help with supper," he said and kissed her forehead.

"Alright then, I'll try and tidy up the house a bit today before I leave tomorrow," said Elizabeth.

"Don't strain yourself, dear, just focus on packing. Let me take you inside," Jacob said.

He helped her up from the bench and escorted her to the door, giving her a quick kiss before walking to the stables. He walked over to his brown mare, Winnie, and stroked her long mane.

"Up for a trip today, girl?" he asked the horse. Winnie exhaled and tossed her mane. He took that to be a yes and fastened the wagon. Jacob climbed up into the seat, gave the reins a shake and set off into town.

Jacob owned a trade business downtown called Hoffner & Clark. His fortune had been made selling groceries up and down the river, exporting wheat and corn and importing sugar from the south. In the last few weeks, Matthew Clark had been responsible for most of the trade operations as the Hoffners coped with their grief. But, the weather this year had been rough on the early crops and Jacob felt he should check in on operations to make sure money would still be coming in. Trips abroad were not inexpensive and as much fortune as Jacob had amassed; he enjoyed the ability to spread his wealth around, often supporting the building of parishes and schools in the city.

As he pulled up to the great brick building, Jacob could see Matthew through the window poring over the record books and counting inventory. Jacob opened the door, and as the bell chimed, Matthew looked up with a smile.

"Jacob! I'm so happy to see you today! How's Elizabeth doing?" Matthew asked. Matthew's youthful face lit up and his blue eyes twinkled as he spoke to his old friend.

"Oh, she's up and about today, off to see her cousin, Miriam tomorrow. I thought I might come in and help out the next few days, see how things are going," said Jacob.

"Not much to worry about here. They say we'll get rain next week which should help the crops. The bills are paid. I would be happy to review the ledgers with you," said Matthew.

Matthew was about ten years younger than Jacob, with sandy reddish-blond hair and gingery freckles. He had a wife, Sylvia, at home and two beautiful girls, Elsa and Hazel. Matthew looked up to Jacob. He had once been his apprentice and risen in his esteem in the past few years to become an equal partner in the grocery business. He had a keen eye, sharp mathematical skills and an honest heart.

Jacob, while not a well-educated man, had learned a lot from reading and traveling the world and was renowned for his fair dealings with others. They made a good team, Hoffner and Clark, and business had prospered. They sold goods as far north as Michigan and imported goods as far south as New Orleans.

Jacob settled down next to Matthew and lost track of

time writing letters and checking figures. He was much relieved that business was going well. As the sky began to darken, he pulled out his pocket watch and realized it was nearly 6:00 p.m. He gave Matthew a pat on the back, promised to be by the next afternoon and left for home.

Elizabeth was upstairs when he arrived, folding dresses and choosing matching bonnets to put into the trunk. She smiled at Jacob as he entered the room and walked over to hug him. He wrapped his strong arms around her frail body and pulled her close, breathing in the scent of her perfume.

"I have a pot of vegetable soup ready if you're hungry," Elizabeth said.

"I know. I smelled it when I walked in. Smells good," said Jacob.

She rested her head on his shoulder, gave him a peck on the cheek.

"I'm almost finished," she said. "Go on down and I'll be there in a minute. I just need to pack a few more things," Elizabeth said.

Jacob went downstairs and began ladling soup into bowls, whistling as he dipped the soup. It had been a fine day and Elizabeth seemed in good spirits. He felt confident he would sleep well that night.

Jacob and Elizabeth spent the evening enjoying the warm soup and chatting about the day. Afterward, they lay in bed reading by lamplight, their feet touching. Elizabeth drifted off to sleep and Jacob took her book from her and set it on the floor. He rolled over and for the first time in weeks, fell asleep without a care.

The next morning, Elizabeth was already up and dressed when he awoke. She leaned down to kiss him, tickling his beard.

"Who's the sleepyhead this morning?" she teased.

Jacob jumped out of bed, dressed and ate some toast, mindful of the time. Elizabeth had to be to the river by 9:00 a.m. They set off in the wagon with the sun shining.

Elizabeth had on one of her best dresses, crimson with lace and had set her hair in curls for the occasion. It seemed her malaise had lifted and she looked every bit the carefree girl he had fallen in love with all those years ago.

When they arrived at the steamer, she was eager to depart.

"Have a good time. Say hello to Miriam for me," Jacob called after her as she boarded the ship.

"I will. I love you," she called after him and blew him a kiss. He pretended to catch it with his hand.

As the ship sailed off down river, he felt a touch of melancholy but shook it off. For the first time in a long time, Jacob felt happy and with newfound energy he set off for work eager to tackle the day ahead.

3

nna's eyes squinted in the sunlight. She blinked and looked up at the trees swaying overhead. It had stopped raining. Her back ached from lying on the hard concrete. She sat up and shook the raindrops out of her long, blonde hair. For a moment, she forgot where she was. She was groggy and everything looked a little blurry.

Something felt off. The hairs on the back of her neck prickled. She froze in place, her heart beating so fast she felt like she might actually die.

She felt the presence of someone behind her. At first she was alarmed, but then a sense of peace washed over her. It was comforting and warm. The wind pressed against her cheek and felt like fingers caressing her tear-stained face. She touched her cheek but nothing was there. She looked behind her and the feeling was gone. Anna could have sworn there was someone actually present. She gathered up her journal and black velvet tote bag and decided it was time to head home.

Anna walked up the steps and took one last look behind her. The traffic was speeding by on the street below. She pulled her coat up around her neck to block the wind and walked down the hill toward her car. Anna jumped the barricade, walked up the gravel drive and unlocked her Honda Civic. Her iPod began to blare a song by Morrissey, "We Hate It When Our Friends Become Successful." A half smile, half smirk formed on her lips. Anna threw her belongings onto the passenger seat and sped away.

Who was Jacob Hoffner? she thought to herself.

She knew he was a distant relative, but it was more than that. Who was he in life and why was she so drawn to his grave? What could it mean? She knew a few facts about him from historical markers around town. What is now the neighborhood of Northside was part of his estate. Hoffner Park, the center of all that is alternative and liberal in Cincinnati was named after him. The gay bar, Jacob's was named after him. Anna had just visited an eclectic deli in Northside called Melt. They have a sandwich called The Hoffner. It's a toasted piece of roast beef, melted Swiss yumminess. Additional information had to exist somewhere for a man with his own sandwich! She tapped her fingers against her teeth in contemplative thought. She pulled into the drive for Oak Ridge Apartments and parked. Anna wondered if Patrick was there – probably not.

He was probably off at an audition flirting with some pretty young actress with well coifed hair without a ketchup stain on her jeans. Anna sighed and mounted the stairs to their apartment. She put the key in the door and shoved. Stupid door was always jamming. She walked down the carpeted hallway and opened her bedroom door. Anna flung herself on the bed, rolled over and buried her head in the pillow. Then she noticed that Patrick had left the internet up on his laptop. Anna rolled out of bed, threw a dirty sweatshirt off of the computer chair and sat down in front of the desk.

Google search for Jacob Hoffner. . . Anna found

something – A Short Biography of Jacob Hoffner. A graduate student named David Mendez had apparently researched Hoffner as part of a project on the founding fathers of Cincinnati. According to his research, Hoffner was a Mason.

Ooh Masons – very DaVinci Code. He must have had a lot of secrets.

Just then, Anna heard the key turn in the lock.

"Anna, you home?"

Patrick had a takeout bag of Chinese food in his hand. *Must be a peace offering,* she thought.

"Yeah, did you get Sweet and Sour Chicken or Chicken Lo Mein this time?" Anna inquired.

"Chicken Lo Mein," Patrick replied.

He smiled and Anna forgot about feeling disgruntled.

"How was your day?" Patrick asked.

"Oh, it was fine. I spent some time outside writing. How was yours?"

Anna didn't elaborate. Patrick found her graveyard wandering to be a little eccentric.

"They're posting callbacks tomorrow. I think I have a shot at one of the younger guys. . ."said Patrick.

He sighed as he slumped down on the couch.

"Can you get the dishes out?" he said lazily.

Anna shot him a look of "Really?" and pulled the plates out of the cabinet.

"Oh yeah, what's the play about?" she asked as she dug in the silverware drawer for a fork.

"It's a love story set during the Civil War," Patrick answered.

"Does this young man have a love interest?" Anna asked with a twinge of jealousy.

"I don't know yet, we'll see. Eat your food. It's getting cold," Patrick said huffily.

Anna slumped down on the couch and flipped channels on the TV until she found the Home Improvement Channel.

"Do you think one day we'll have our own place with an open floor plan and Venetian blinds?" Anna asked.

She swooned at the DIY makeover on the set.

"Not when I get my big break and we get our studio apartment in New York," Patrick said as he slurped a noodle up.

Anna stopped talking and ate the rest of her meal in silence.

New York – Patrick had big dreams of being on Broadway. This was not a dream Anna shared. She longed for ocean waves, driving down back roads with the windows down and the wind blowing in her hair. The idea of living in a tiny, cramped New York apartment made her cringe. But, as she had done so often before in life, Anna swallowed her dreams with the noodles and pretended that New York was the place to be.

The couple silently watched back to back sitcom reruns of *How I Met Your Mother* until Patrick started to snore on the couch. Anna crept out from under his arm stealth mode, walked quietly down the hall and slunk under the covers in their bed. She tossed and turned thinking about Jacob and writing and all of the dreams she didn't share in the light of day.

The next morning Anna awoke to the sound of the garbage truck rumbling down the street. She peeked one eye out from under the covers and stared at the alarm clock "8:00", which was early for her. Anna walked downstairs and found a note from Patrick explaining that he was running to Starbucks and then over to the playhouse to see if he was on the callback list.

Anna pulled the laptop back out and tried to write. No, this wasn't going to work. She envisioned herself staring all day at the blank screen trying to write between watching old episodes of *The Brady Bunch* and thinking of new ways to procrastinate with laundry. She needed to go back to the graveyard. She wasn't finished there. She was on to something. She felt the muse calling to her – or something along those lines.

Anna ran upstairs and threw on some old jeans and a Nine Inch Nails t-shirt from college. She ran a brush through her hair, and slapped on some lipstick. Part of her wanted to wait for Patrick to get back with some Starbucks, but when she had an idea brewing, she couldn't let it go.

Back at the cemetery, the rain had left a wet sheen on all of the trees and leaves. The sun was out with just a few thin clouds along the horizon. Anna tromped over to her spot at the top of the stairs and plopped down with her notepad.

WWJD – What would Jacob do?

She snorted at herself because she thought it was funny.

"I don't know. What would I do?" she heard a voice she didn't recognize say.

Anna jumped and looked around.

"Hello?" she said meekly.

"You come here a lot," said the voice.

Anna looked down the staircase – no one was there.

She turned around and saw a faint shadowy figure of a man. It was almost as if he was made of television static. He had a long beard, was wearing a hat, a suitcoat and dark trousers.

"Let me introduce myself. My name is Jacob. I believe you've been looking for me."

4

Matthew was in the backroom when Jacob arrived. He was counting the bags of wheat and preparing them for shipment. He greeted Jacob warmly and asked about Elizabeth's departure. Jacob updated him on the morning's events and then set to work, helping Matthew count and move bags out to the wagons. He enjoyed the physical labor of it all and it helped keep his mind off the quiet days ahead. Elizabeth was to return in two weeks, hopefully much refreshed and in good spirits after visiting with her cousin.

Miriam and Elizabeth had been very close as young girls and wrote each other often. Miriam had lost her son, young Edward, in his infancy. So, they had much in common and he hoped that her friendship would be a great comfort to his wife.

Jacob worked into the late afternoon. Around 5:00, he asked Matthew if he would be attending the meeting of Masonic Lodge 234 later that evening. Matthew replied that yes, he intended to be there after putting the girls to bed.

Jacob, as a Master Mason, had recruited Matthew into the Order when Matthew was a young man. Masonic Order 234 was one of the largest in Ohio and the largest in Cincinnati. Jacob's father, John Hoffner, had been a lifetime Mason member in Pennsylvania, and Jacob proudly carried on the family tradition.

After closing up shop, Jacob climbed into the wagon, tired with sore muscles from heaving grain all afternoon. He rode home to retrieve his apron, cape and candles before heading to the lodge on Washington Street. As he pulled up to the brick building, he saw a crowd of wagons circling the block and the oil lanterns burning on the outside greeting the Order inside for the meeting.

He gave the secret password and was admitted into the dark interior. He walked in and immediately ran into his dear friend, Henry Marsden. Henry had been a childhood friend who was married to Antoinette Marsden, a dear friend of Elizabeth's. He hadn't seen Henry in some weeks. They gave each other the Masonic handshake and went inside to take their seats.

"Do you plan to go abroad anytime soon?" asked Henry.

"Indeed, I would like to get to England sometime within the next year. I'm hoping to buy some more statuary for my gardens and to see if there are any other plants I can transport that will withstand the voyage," said Jacob.

"Excellent. If I can find a way to join you, I shall. Antoinette has been talking of going out West next year, so I will see if I can find the time," said Henry.

Jacob enjoyed the fraternity of his brotherhood and especially enjoyed the moments of socialization before the meeting was called to order.

Jacob led his way to the front to assist with the convening of the meeting and the introduction of new men into the Order.

"We now convene the meeting of the Masonic Order

234. What old business do we have to discuss?" said the Grandmaster, a man by the name of Nicholas Brundy.

A member came forward to discuss the repairs to the roof, some charity work they planned to do for a church for the Easter holidays and the treasurer gave a report on the budget. Next, came Jacob's favorite part, the initiation of new members. He donned his cape and began reciting the secret words. All of the members sat in rapt attention. Jacob was well respected amongst the men and was one of the highest members in the Order. They inducted three new men that night, chanting the ancient words all together in a humming uniform sound that filled the lamp lit room. Time passed quickly as the men performed the ancient rites. The air from the chanting warmed the room and Jacob loosened his collar. Sweat beaded on his brow. He brushed it away with his sleeve. The men spoke, "So mote it be," and the meeting was adjourned.

"Henry, wait a moment," said Jacob. He grabbed the arm of his friend as he began to walk out of the room.

"Yes, Jacob?" said Henry.

"I'm thinking of having a few friends over tomorrow night for dinner. It's a bit lonely in the house with Elizabeth gone and I would enjoy the company," said Jacob.

"I would love to. I could be there around 7:00. Shall I bring anything?" asked Henry.

"I have bread, potatoes and a roast. If you would like to bring some wine that would be great" said Jacob.

"Sounds good. I shall see you at 7:00 tomorrow, old friend," said Henry.

Jacob walked out into the night air, dabbing his brow with a handkerchief and enjoying the feel of coolness. Matthew walked up behind him, startling him.

"Excellent recitation tonight, Jacob. Always a good meeting when you're present," said Matthew.

"Thank you. I appreciate it," said Jacob.

"Shall I see you at work in the morning?" asked

Matthew.

"Certainly. I look forward to it," said Jacob.

Jacob walked back to the wagon. It had been a long day. He drove home, yawning and craving rest. As he pulled into the drive, he got out to open the black wrought iron gates so his horse could pass through, closed them, put the horse in the barn and walked through the garden in the moonlight. He stared down at the tulips next to Elizabeth's favorite fountain and felt a pang of loneliness. As he entered the house, he began to strip off his sweat-soaked clothes and put a pot on the stove to boil water for a hot bath. He bathed quickly, put on his nightclothes and blew out the lamp.

13 more days until her return, he thought as he drifted off to sleep.

The next morning Jacob rose before breakfast and got out his pen and ink. He had decided to write to Miriam to check on his wife. She had not yet arrived on the steamer, but by the time the letter posted, she should be there.

"Dear Elizabeth, I hope you are having a lovely time with Miriam. Give her my best," he began.

A few minutes later, he sealed the envelope, placed it in his satchel to mail later at the post office and got ready for work. As the sun came up, he decided to take his tea out to the garden to relax before the day began. He looked at his reflection in the pool and noticed how old he was starting to look. He was nearing 40 and the lines were beginning to show on his face, a thick line of salt and pepper was evident in his hair. Elizabeth said he looked distinguished. But, he didn't feel as old as he was beginning to look. There was so much more he wanted to do with his life.

He wanted to tour Europe again, particularly Italy. Italy was so beautiful and had a more temperate climate than England. His travels usually took him to England. It was there that he was conferred his Masonic degrees by the founding organization. But, three times he had been to Italy and bought many sculptures. He had heard the artwork in Greece was remarkable and hoped to go there and show Elizabeth the sites. He had generally gone alone or with friends. He pulled out his pocket watch and looked at the time. He needed to go. He planned to put in a full day at the office, stop by the post office and return home for his impromptu dinner party.

The day passed slowly. All of the bills had been paid and the inventory was counted. He spent most of the day writing letters to merchants and filling out invoices. It was tedious and his least favorite part of the job. As night fell, his mood brightened as he thought of his friends coming over. Henry planned to come, as well as Matthew and his friend, George, who lived down the street. He imagined a lively night of conversation, charades, drinking and general merriment.

After stopping at the post office, he hurried home and tidied the house. At 7:00 p.m., the bell rang. The smell of roast beef and warm bread filled the house. Jacob opened the door to find Henry and showed him to the dining room. Next came Matthew followed by George. They ate the feast in relative silence, each commenting on what a grand meal it was for a gentleman to prepare. Henry reminded them that Jacob had started out as an apprentice to a baker and knew his way about a kitchen.

"A lucky lady that Elizabeth," said George. "I know nary a man who can cook like you do, Jacob. My wife must feed me three square meals a day. If anything were to happen to her, by God, I'd starve to death!" he laughed.

They retired to the drawing room, lit some cigars and pulled out a bottle of wine. Matthew made a joke asking if Jacob had any lady magazines. Jacob gave him a playful shove and went to the kitchen to find more wine.

Just then, a knock came at the door. Jacob was surprised. He had not invited anyone else to the soiree. Perhaps, the neighbors had heard the commotion and had come to complain. When he opened the door, he found a policeman standing at the door, with a telegram in his hand.

"I hate to be the one to tell you this, sir. But, it seems there has been an accident. The steamer, the W.R. Carter, sir has exploded on the Mississippi en route to New Orleans. I'm afraid there are no survivors," said the policeman.

He looked down afraid to see Jacob's reaction. Jacob stared at the policeman, not understanding the words.

"But, my wife. My wife was on that ship," said Jacob. He stared blankly, not speaking, not closing the door.

"Are you alright sir? I know this must be a terrible shock," said the policeman.

Henry came to the door. "What is it Jacob, what's happened? Jacob?"

Jacob held onto the beam of the doorway.

"Elizabeth!" he screamed. "No, no, no, no!!!!!!!"

Jacob cried and fell to his knees. He couldn't catch his breath. He could feel the buzz of the wine in his veins. Henry questioned the policeman for details. When? How? What was the cause? Jacob sat on the floor. Matthew ran to help him to a chair. George filled the water basin and patted his face trying to restore the color. The door closed. Henry must have finished speaking to the policeman and sent him away. The merriment of the evening had come to a halt. Henry offered to stay. Matthew and George said they would leave and call in the morning. Jacob felt numb. His world was crashing around him and he wanted not to think, not to breathe, not to be.

5

Anna stepped backward, nearly tripping on a tree root and gasped.

"But. . . it can't be. I must have fallen asleep. This must be some kind of dream."

"I assure you, I'm quite real," said the apparition.

Anna closed her eyes and opened them again. He was still there – he looked to be almost six feet tall, with a long white beard, receding hairline, and kind, grey eyes. He was wearing a long black suit coat with a vest underneath and black pants. In his right hand, he was carrying a cane. He appeared to be almost solid except for a transparent quality to his face. She could see through it to the pine trees that stood behind him.

"What do you want?" Anna asked, knees trembling.

"I think the question is not so much, what do I want, but what do you want? You're the one who visits me in such distress," replied the gentle stranger.

"I just. . .your grave, it's so peaceful. I feel like I can think here. The statue of your wife is so beautiful. It makes me feel like this is a place full of love," replied Anna.

"Oh, Elizabeth was quite the beauty. Every night as

we would lie in the covers trying to keep warm, I would hold her in my arms and stare at her in amazement that the likes of her would spend her days with me. She was taken too soon that one," said Jacob.

"That sounds so nice. I've never had anyone love me like that," Anna sighed and found a spot on the ground. "Why are you appearing to me now?" Anna asked. "When I've come here so many times before? Am I going crazy?"

"No, child," Jacob replied. "It seemed to me when you were last here that you were struggling to find your place in this world. I know how difficult that can be. I, myself, had difficulty fitting in with my contemporaries. I was a bit of what you would call a radical – more apt to quote Thoreau than to follow the status quo." Jacob chuckled.

"I always wanted to leave something behind in this world too, to have people remember me after I was gone. But, it seems that the only person to remember me after all these years is you. And that's why I've come. I was hoping we might work out a mutually beneficial arrangement," said Jacob.

"What kind of arrangement?"

"You, Anna, are my family and as such, I would like to bequeath something to you," said Jacob.

Anna crossed her legs and stared in rapt attention.

"I'm listening. . ." she said.

"As you may know, I was once a prominent Mason in this community. I belonged to the Masonic Order for many years, often traveling abroad to receive my Masonic degrees," said Jacob.

"I read something along those lines," said Anna.

"I had always hoped to leave a legacy of sorts. I feel I am dead and gone but there is nothing to remember me by," said Jacob.

"Oh, but there is, there's a park where your house stood and why, they even have a sandwich named after you!" said Anna.

Jacob chuckled and leaned against the statue of his wife.

"Is that the legacy you want to leave, my dear? I think we both long for something more. What I have in mind is more personal and I need you to help me pull it off," said Jacob.

"Why me?" said Anna.

"Well, you're a writer, aren't you? And from your musings on my steps, I gather you have some time on your hands. It might even cheer your spirits. Up for a little intrigue?" said Jacob.

Anna tried to process what was happening and felt the grass beneath her fingers, still trying to determine if this was all real. What did she have to lose, really? Maybe she was crazy. Maybe this was all a hallucination. She was depressed, after all. She closed her eyes again. Nope, he was still there.

"So, you were saying, something about the Masons?" said Anna.

"Yes, have you heard of the Hoffner Lodge?" said Jacob.

"I have. It's on the other end of town. They have yoga classes there and rent it out for parties," said Anna.

Jacob rolled his eyes, "Well, it was once the greatest Masonic Order this state has ever known. I helped build it and I have something there I would like you to retrieve for me," said Jacob.

"On the second floor, there is a large hall with a stage. In that room, there is a closet. One of the floorboards in the closet has a notch in it. If you pull on the notch, the floorboard will come up. I've hidden something there and I want you to find it," said Jacob.

"But, what is it?" Anna asked impatiently.

"You'll know when you find it," said Jacob.

"How am I going to pull this off? There are people in there. I can't just go wandering about. I might get arrested," said Anna.

"For pulling on floorboards?" said Jacob, "I doubt that. You'll be fine."

Anna wrung her hands and rubbed them on her knees. She rubbed her hands over her face. What would Patrick think when she told him? He would probably try to admit her to a mental institution. Of course, she didn't have to tell him. With that thought, a small smile spread across her face. He had his auditions and his New York dreams. What did she have really?

She liked to dabble in yoga. Maybe she could take a class, slip out for a minute, creep upstairs. It could work.

"I'll do it," she heard herself say.

"Good. I was hoping you would say that," and with that Jacob slowly faded out of focus.

"Wait. . .I have more questions!" Anna called out to the empty air.

She found herself alone again amongst the trees with a lump in her throat. Her Converse shoes digging into the ground, she ran her fingers through her greasy hair in exasperation. Her refuge of solitude suddenly seemed too quiet. She stared out over the hill at the passing traffic of the street below and tried to ground herself. She suddenly felt frightened that she was losing her mind and tears welled up in her eyes. Maybe she should go home and sleep. This would all make more sense after a nap. She fumbled in her pocket for her keys.

As she stood up, she braced herself against the closest pine tree and walked slowly back to the car. Her hands were shaking. The keys jangled as she tried to fit them into the lock of her Civic. She finally got the door open and sat for a moment with her head leaning against the steering wheel. Yes, some rest and a solid meal - that would clear her head. She put the car into drive and drove down the hill listening to the gravel crunch under the tires, staring into the trees paranoid about who else might be listening and watching.

When she arrived home, she threw herself on the bed

and buried her head under the downy pillow. Her head throbbed. She could see the sun disappearing over the horizon outside her bedroom window. Anna squinted her eyes and went over to close the blinds. Within a few minutes, she was asleep.

Anna awoke to find Patrick bending over her, his dark hair brushing her forehead. She jumped.

"You all right? I was just waking you up to tell you dinner is ready. I made cheeseburgers," said Patrick.

"What time is it?" Anna asked with a yawn.

"It's about 6:30. How long have you been asleep?" asked Patrick.

"I don't know. . .since 3:00 maybe," she responded.

"Well get up. We need to celebrate. I got the part!" Patrick said excitedly.

"Oh good, that's great, honey. I'm happy for you," Anna said with a forced grin.

"I'll be out in a minute," she said. Anna walked into the bathroom and splashed cold water on her face. She stared into the mirror.

"Get it together, Anna." she said to her wide-eyed reflection. Anna pulled her hair into a ponytail, dried her face and went out to the dining room.

"Smells good. I'm hungry," she said to Patrick, biting into her cheeseburger.

"Auditions went so well, today. I nailed it. I knew I had it by the way the director smiled at me. What's the matter, Anna, you look like something's wrong?" Patrick asked.

Patrick's excitement seemed to wane.

"Oh no, I'm just tired. This is exciting news. I can't wait for the show. I'll be right in front cheering you on," Anna said.

She busied herself with eating to avoid talking. Her mind was swirling with a montage of the day's events – Jacob, the lodge, the quest. She wiped her mouth with her napkin.

"This was good, honey. Thank you. You know I'm not feeling so well. I think I might just watch TV in the bed and turn in early tonight," Anna said.

"Alright. I'm going to stay up and start memorizing my lines. Rehearsal starts in two days and I don't want to be one of those amateurs that are calling 'line' every five minutes."

Patrick walked over to hug her. "Let me know if you need anything," he said as she closed the bedroom door.

Anna switched on the TV and found some re-runs of *The Cosby Show*. She had no desire to watch it, just wanted the background noise. She pushed back her cuticles, breathing deeply.

Maybe I am crazy, she thought. *Maybe I fell asleep at the cemetery and dreamed all of that up.*

Still, a nagging curiosity filled her mind with doubt. She had to go to that lodge and see for herself. She had an old yoga mat somewhere in the back of one of her closets. Sweats and a t-shirt would do. She was supposed to work a shift at the FedEx shipping facility in the morning, but she had the afternoon free.

Anna pulled out her laptop to see if there were any yoga classes in the afternoon. 2:00 Gentle Yoga. Instructor's name was Maureen. That will work. She pushed the worry aside and escaped into the TV show. Bill was trying to get Theo to do better in school. Anna laughed along with the laugh track. Yes, yoga – it seemed time for her to stretch beyond her comfort zone.

Who knows? Maybe she would find what she was looking for. Maybe nothing would be there. Either way, tomorrow seemed like the dawning of a new day, full of more excitement than Anna had felt in a long, long time.

6

The next morning when Jacob awoke, Henry was sitting in a chair next to his bedside. Jacob jumped, not expecting him to be there and then upon remembering why he was there, his face crumbled in despair. Henry offered to make him some tea and Jacob nodded accepting the kind request like a small child feeling lost. He sipped the tea slowly, and asked Henry for more details about what the policeman had learned about the accident. It seemed that the boilers had exploded, engulfing the ship in fire and burning the passenger section before help could arrive.

Oh the horror of his dear Elizabeth perishing in such a painful and terrifying way. He shouldn't have let her go. He should have sensed that something would happen.

Henry asked if Jacob would like him to stay the remainder of the day. Jacob declined, claiming that he would be alright. He did not rise to show Henry to the door, but chose to remain in the bed with the blinds drawn.

For hours, he stared blankly at the wall, didn't eat or move to get up. He simply couldn't imagine a future without Elizabeth. He debated what his next move should be. Obviously, there was no body, but he should arrange some type of memorial service. Elizabeth had only two living close relatives, a sister named Sarah who lived in Indiana and her daughter, Molly. Jacob thought of sending a telegram, but decided it would be best to tell them in person. That was the right thing to do. As night fell, he slowly got up and went downstairs, had a bit of bread and milk and then retreated back to his bed once more.

Two days passed with Jacob in much the same state. Then, Matthew arrived and helped Jacob dress, made him some eggs and encouraged him to go visit Elizabeth's sister. Jacob sat for a time in the garden, tears streaming down his face as he looked at the beautiful gardens he had cultivated for his wife.

He went back inside, packed an overnight bag, hitched up the wagon and began the long journey to Bloomingdale. The day was cloudy with the sun peeking out of the clouds for a couple of minutes every few hours. He bypassed the heavily congested main roads in favor of the dirt back country roads. The stillness in the air, accompanied only by the sound of hooves was soothing to his mind.

A few hours in, he stopped to rest, drink water and eat a sandwich he had packed. He entered Parke County as the sun was beginning to set. He shook the reins to get the horse to pick up speed as he wanted to arrive at Sarah's by nightfall.

The Hoffners had only visited Indiana to visit Sarah a handful of times. Generally, Sarah traveled to Cincinnati to see her sister and enjoy the hustle and bustle of city life. Elizabeth would take her on sightseeing tours and they would laugh and giggle and stay up late hours in the living room talking by lamplight. Jacob was not looking forward to giving her the news.

Coming around a curve in the road, Jacob spotted a covered bridge ahead. The words "Jackson Bridge" were painted brightly above the bright white structure. Jacob stopped the wagon before entering and stepped down. He walked down the embankment and stared at the rocky creek below. He sat down for a while, motionless, listening to the water trickle over the rocks. The horse whinnied with impatience, not understanding why they had stopped.

It's almost dark, Jacob thought. *No one would come find me if I jumped into the cold, dark water. No one would come looking for me.*

He had no one really. Elizabeth was gone. All his children were dead in the grave. What reason was there to continue on? Or maybe, he thought, he could walk into the long dark overhang of the bridge and lie down. Perhaps another wagon would come by and trample him, not seeing him in the darkness.

An ache, a heaviness hung on him. He thought of floating off downstream and joining his Elizabeth in heaven.

He closed his eyes. He was tired from the day of travel. Memories floated through his mind – memories of Elizabeth, how she had struggled with having children only to lose them during childbirth. He thought of Matthew and whether he would be able to run the business alone if Jacob left it to him. He thought of his brother Masons and the fraternity they shared.

As he gazed out at the moonlight, he thought of a phrase from one of the Masonic rituals,

The light of a Master Mason is darkness visible.

He wasn't sure what it meant. He looked at the outlines of the trees in the darkness, the shimmer of the moonlight on the creek. *Darkness was visible – was the light to be found within?* He thought of Elizabeth. If she had gone with him, she would have found it romantic to sit here in the moonlight looking out beyond the covered bridge. She always found the beauty and light even on her darkest days. She had been brave to go see Miriam after suffering such a loss. *What right did he have to sit there and not find the strength to go on?* He took a deep breath and stood up. He was still filled with sadness, but the suicidal fantasies had subsided, and he was resolute in his mission to find Sarah and give her the news.

He continued on the path until he found the turnoff for Sarah's cabin. As Jacob approached, he could make out the outline of the log frame and smell the smoke billowing from the chimney. He saw a woman walk out onto the porch, a shotgun in her hand.

"Who's there?" she called out.

"It's Jacob, Sarah," he responded.

She put the gun down on the porch swing and walked out to meet him. Sarah carried his bag and helped him maneuver his way along the dark stones leading to the covered porch.

"Molly's asleep," she explained opening the door. "Is everything alright? Where's Elizabeth?" she asked.

He motioned for her to come inside and sit down. Sarah sat in a wooden rocking chair near the window and covered herself with an afghan. The home was modestly furnished but warm. The last embers of a fire were crackling in the fireplace.

Sarah was two years older than Elizabeth. Her light brown hair was pulled back into a bun, tendrils escaped and curled around her ears. Her face looked weathered, likely from managing a homestead on her own as a single mother. Her husband, Ronald, had died from cholera shortly after Molly was born. For some reason, she looked more pale and tired than usual. It was probably the late hour and the unexpected visit, Jacob thought. He wasn't sure where to begin, so he just said it.

"There's been an accident, Sarah," Jacob said. "Elizabeth went on a steamship to visit Miriam a few days ago. The boilers caught fire en route. There were no survivors," Jacob said quietly.

Sarah didn't speak for a few minutes. "Is there anything I can do?" she asked.

She doubled over in a coughing fit and then sat up, sadness in her eyes, and stared at Jacob with compassion.

"I'm so sorry for your loss, Jacob. I know you loved Elizabeth very much. She was very lucky to have you," said Sarah.

"I'm sorry for your loss. I know you two were very close, especially as children," said Jacob.

Sarah invited him to stay the night and went to the guest bedroom to lay out an extra quilt. Jacob retired to the room, took off his boots and put out the light. Jacob could hear Sarah in the other room softly crying. She had put up a brave front for him, but she was cut in two by the loss of her sister. She was a tough girl, Sarah.

The next morning, Jacob awoke to a small hand tugging on his beard.

"Wake up, Uncle Jacob!" a little voice implored.

He opened his eyes to see his five year old niece, Molly, jumping up and down on the bed. She grabbed his arm and tried to tug him into a sitting position.

"Mommy made pancakes! Come on Uncle Jacob, breakfast time!"

He groggily stood up and watched her bounce out the door. He dressed and went into the kitchen to find Molly sitting at the oak table pouring maple syrup on her pancakes with childlike glee. Sarah was at the stove, flipping pancakes in the cast iron skillet and making a plate for Jacob.

"Good morning, Jacob," said Sarah with no trace of the despair of the night before aside from the sad eyes.

"Good morning, Sarah. This is quite a treat. Thank you," Jacob said.

"Uncle Jacob, will you play marbles with me after breakfast?" Molly asked.

She was very excited to have a visitor, and Sarah had not shared the sad news about her aunt with her yet.

"Certainly, sweetheart," Jacob said rumpling her curly hair.

Her round face was covered in syrup and her smile lit up the whole room. He had always loved children, and they had tried so hard to have some of their own, but the babies never made it. For the first time all week, Molly had made him smile, and it felt good.

He helped Sarah clean the dishes and then spent the morning hours playing with Molly. She giggled and squealed as they played tag. She accused him of cheating at marbles. She hid in the same spot over and over when they played hide and seek, every time astounded that he found her. It was nice and made the moment on the bridge seem long ago and far away.

After lunch, he packed his things and told them he had better get going. Molly pouted and begged him not to go. He took Sarah aside and told her that he needed to get back to arrange a memorial service. She went to her room and brought back a locket of her mother's and asked that it be buried next to Elizabeth's headstone. Jacob assured her that he would see to it. He reached down and gave Molly a big hug and spun her around. He kissed Sarah on the cheek and made his way home.

As he passed through Jackson Bridge once more, he felt lighter than when he passed that way the first time. In his heart, the darkness was still visible, but he also felt the visit had stoked the dying embers of his inner fire and a flame shot up through the darkness.

7

The alarm clock blared into Anna's ear. She grumpily reached over and smacked it, opened her eyes and glared at the sunlight coming in through the blinds. Rolling over, she stared at the time, 7:00 a.m., time to get ready for work. She pulled back the covers and stumbled out to the kitchen to turn on the coffee maker. She looked around, wondering where Patrick could be. Once the coffee started to brew, she went back to her room to dig through the laundry basket for her work clothes. Her khakis were reasonably clean; the FedEx polo shirt wrinkled but respectable looking. She took a brush through her hair, brushed her teeth, laced her steel-toed boots and was out the door in less than ten minutes.

The drive to work took about 20 minutes. She listened to old songs from high school along the way – some Depeche Mode, The Cure and Toad the Wet Sprocket. As she pulled into the parking lot, the facility was already alive with people bustling about getting packages ready to ship out that morning. Anna's job was very basic. Boxes came down a conveyer belt and as each one slid by, she inserted a ream of paper. It was mundane and mind numbing. She hated it, but for someone with her erratic work history and a boyfriend with an unstable career, it was what she had to do for the time being. It kept food on the table and paid the bills.

When she walked in, Brad, her 20 year old boss, told her to get to her position immediately. He really enjoyed ordering people around and had his sights on upper management. Already, he was developing a beer belly and receding hairline. Anna imagined he would grow up to be one of those sad, middle-aged men who spend their weekends at the bar complaining about their ex-wife and reminiscing about their high school football days. She hated Brad. It didn't help that he was younger than her. That really got under her skin. She gritted her teeth at him, swiped her badge at the time clock and took her post.

Most days, time dragged at the warehouse. She would count the minutes until her 10 minute break. But, today, especially was unbearable. All she could think about was going to the Hoffner Lodge later and looking under that floorboard. What could it be? She stared down, box coming down the line, put paper in box – box, paper, box, paper. There had to be more to life than box, paper. She yawned and looked at the clock. Five minutes had passed. It was going to be a long morning. Two hours later, it was time for her break. She went searching for her only friend at work, a little old lady named Midge.

Midge had worked at the warehouse for 20 years and was like a surrogate grandmother to Anna. Midge was already in the break room when she arrived, banging on the snack machine to get a bag of Cheez-It's to fall out.

"Darn you, Cheez-It's," Midge yelled at the machine.

She was a feisty old gal, 68 years old, eligible to retire but not wanting to give up her routine.

"Hey chickadee, How you doing this morning?" said Midge.

"Oh alright, do you need some help with that machine?" Anna said and slammed her fist against it.

The Cheez-It's fell to the bottom.

"Thank you Anna. I was about to unleash some ugly on that there contraption," said Midge.

"I don't doubt it," said Anna.

They sat down on the hard plastic chairs and Anna watched Midge devour her snack. Anna wasn't about to tell her about her secret mission. They weren't particularly close, but Anna liked having someone to talk to at work. But, Anna did tell her about trying out yoga class that afternoon.

"Ooh girl, you're braver than me. I'd never get this old body into a bendy position," said Midge.

"It's gentle yoga, Midge. I bet you could do it," said Anna.

"I don't know, child. You'll see when you get old. You don't use it, you lose it. More power to ya," said Midge.

Just then, the whistle blew and it was back to two more hours of box, paper, box, paper.

Anna raced home after her shift was over, relieved to be free of the place at last. She dug through her closet.

"Where are you yoga mat?" she said out loud to herself.

Sweatpants, candy wrappers, old board games, shoes – she really needed to clean one day. After pulling out a basket of winter boots, she spied the purple foam. Aha – yoga mat. She yanked it out from under the boots and wiped the dust off of it. Then she shimmied out of her work clothes, threw on sweats and a t-shirt and tied her hair back in a ponytail. She walked by the mirror, glanced at her reflection and stopped for a minute. Then she turned and went into the bathroom and dug through the top drawer. Finding some lip gloss, she applied it and examined her pout in the mirror.

There, that's better, she thought.

Then she skipped out the door and ran out to the car. A few minutes later, she walked back in the door, grabbed her car keys and the yoga mat and was off to the lodge for real, this time. She turned the radio dial actually hoping to hear some new music. She stopped when she heard Taylor Swift belting out "Shake It Off" and sang along. As she neared the lodge, she turned the radio down in order to hear the GPS directions better – in 1000 feet, you will arrive at your destination. She pulled up to the curb, got out, fed the meter and then looked up at the towering, brick building before her.

At the top of the building, the words "Hoffner Lodge 1855" were imprinted in an arch pattern. The rest of the building was a dark orange brick color. It was three stories high with several large windows facing out to the street. Anna saw a young girl with dreadlocks getting out of her car, yoga mat in hand. Anna walked a few paces behind her, not wanting to look like a newbie at the yoga studio.

As she entered the building, she noticed on the placard that several businesses now shared the space. There was a Buddhist meditation center, a belly dancing troupe, a yoga studio, a bike shop, and an art gallery. It seemed like a gathering space for artists of all types. There was a slightly musty smell that old buildings have, but the interior was freshly painted with modern art hung in the corridor. Anna thought for a moment that Jacob would be proud that the space continued to be a place for friends to meet and engage in rituals.

Anna followed the girl with brown dreadlocks to the third room on the first floor and found eight other women, laying mats on the floor, picking up Styrofoam bricks and grabbing some type of rope that looked like a Boy Scout belt off of a shelf. Anna sat down on the floor and pretended to stretch. She gazed around and saw women of various ages – a few toned, tanned college girls, some aging hippies with long gray hair and a couple of middle-aged women in sweats who looked like they were trying exercise for the very first time. The instructor looked to be about twenty-five, was waif thin, had long 'black hair tied into a bun on the top of her head and was busy lighting candles and choosing music.

"Welcome class. Today we are going to be practicing gentle yoga. Just try whatever poses feel best to you. If at any time, you are not feeling the pose, you can feel free to go into child's pose and remain there as long as you need. Now let's take a big stretch overhead," said the instructor.

The class dutifully stretched their arms to the sky, and then stretched to the right and the left. Anna contemplated how she was going to get upstairs. She hadn't thought this through.

"And I'll meet you in downward dog," said the instructor.

Anna clumsily formed herself into an arc, realizing her heels didn't touch the floor like the other yogis. Maybe she could pretend to go get water. But, she had brought in a full water bottle – stupid. As she sunk down into pigeon pose, she started gulping down water like a man lost in the desert. Water dribbled down her chin. The instructor squinted her eyes and gave her a strange look and then sighed. By the time they were back in downward dog, Anna had gulped down three quarters of her water bottle. She tried to form an expression on her face that suggested, "Man, I'm thirsty," and got up and walked out the door with her water bottle as the class balanced in tree pose.

Walking quickly and quietly down the hall, Anna stopped to look behind her to see if anyone had followed her. All was quiet except for the echo of her own footsteps. She located the large wooden spiral staircase at the end of the hall and began to ascend to the second floor. It had been a long time since she had attempted yoga and her legs were a little wobbly. Twice she nearly tripped going up the stairs, but made it to the top unscathed. The second floor turned out to be a large open space with windows on all sides. Anna walked over to the window and looked out at the city below, the treetops budding showing the first signs of spring. There was a stage at the far corner of the room and a small kitchen area.

They must rent this out for weddings, she thought.

She looked about for a closet and saw what looked to be a coat closet on the right side of the stage. She tiptoed over to it and opened the door inch by inch; paranoid that someone would come up and demand to know what she was doing. The closet was full of metal folding chairs; there must have been fifty in there.

Crap, she thought.

She started pulling them out a stack at a time and set them on the floor. Luckily, all her time hefting boxes at the warehouse had given her a good deal of upper body strength, so she accomplished the task within a matter of minutes. She knelt down on her hands and knees and felt the floorboards. It was just a floor. She began to feel like a fool or a crazy person. Her eyes welled up with tears.

It must be here. It must, she thought.

She folded her body forward into child's pose and tried to take deep breaths. As her fingers stretched in front of her, her fingernail caught on a notch in the wood. She rubbed it with her fingertip and discovered it was a small hole that her finger fit inside. She pulled and the floorboard began to lift. Underneath, was a small box, no bigger than an Altoids tin. On the outside was engraved,

"Seek and ye shall find. Ask and it shall be given unto you. Knock and it shall be opened unto you" ~ Matthew 7:7.

She knocked on the outside of the small metal box and inside was a solitary skeleton key. On the oval top part of the key was the word, "Journey." That was all. Anna slipped the key into her pocket, put the box back under the floorboard and pushed it down with her foot. She looked around nervously, but the air was still. Hurriedly, she put the folding chairs back in the closet and closed the door.

She rushed downstairs, refilled her water bottle at the

water fountain and returned to yoga class as they were starting savasana. She lay down on the floor breathing deeply, trying to still her racing heartbeat. She thought of how odd it was that she was lying in corpse pose, holding a skeleton key that belonged to a ghost. It was delightfully morbid. She sat up, put her hands in prayer position and whispered "Namaste" along with the class. Then she rolled up her yoga mat, put the equipment away and sauntered out of the room.

As she walked outside into the sunshine, she pulled the key out of her pocket to verify that it was really there. *"Journey" – what did that mean? What did the key unlock and why did Jacob want her to get it?* She ran her fingers over the cool, metal edges and slipped the key back in her pocket. She opened the car and sat down for a minute before closing the door, trying to decide her next steps.

The thought of returning to the graveyard filled her with both excitement and fear. Everything was happening so quickly and she wasn't sure where it was leading. What if Jacob was some kind of evil spirit sent to provoke her into committing dark deeds? No, she had always felt so warm and safe at his gravesite. She couldn't believe that his intentions could be anything other than pure. But, she felt that perhaps he had made a mistake in choosing her. There was nothing special about her. Maybe he simply chose her because she had so much time on her hands and was likely to take direction from a being in the afterlife.

She closed the car door and started the ignition. She didn't know why he chose her and she didn't know what he wanted her to do. But, there was only one way to find out.

8

The week that followed was busy. There were meetings with the police, steamship company representatives, and lawyers. A death certificate was filed and Jacob planned a memorial service at Pine Grove Cemetery. He had helped with the landscaping of the cemetery and it was considered by many to be one of the most beautiful cemeteries in the Midwest. Elizabeth had requested a spot on a hill so she could watch over her loved ones. Jacob found her the perfect spot in the center of a grove of trees. He had purchased the spot many years ago as a family plot and small markers were placed next to the graves of their infants.

Elizabeth was not to have a casket. There was no body to be found, but he buried the locket along with some of her letters in a tin box next to a fine marble headstone. He commissioned a sculptor to construct a statue resembling Elizabeth to place in the middle. When he finished, the white marble was breathtaking. Elizabeth would have loved it. The memorial service was small, mainly neighbors, some friends of Elizabeth's. Many of their relatives lived far away or were already gone. But, several sent letters of condolence. The few people who did attend were overcome with grief, enfolding Jacob in their arms and offering to bring over food. She was a beautiful lady and many hearts broke at the news of her passing. People who barely knew her – the postman, the butcher came to pay their respects and wept openly. They spoke of her kindness and her smile and of how much she had loved Jacob.

Jacob often woke feeling like an elephant was on his chest or a knife was cutting his heart. It was hard to breathe. He missed her so much. He would try to remember the sound of her voice and her smile. He was afraid the memory of her would fade away. Every night he would light a candle and say a prayer for her. He was not a religious man, but he began to hope that there was a heaven. If there was, his Elizabeth was most surely there. He would give anything to see her, talk to her, and hold her one last time. There was so much he wanted to say to her.

For a while, he visited the gravesite daily, often talking to the statue as if it was Elizabeth herself. This gave him great comfort and made him feel less alone. He brought her flowers from their gardens – daisies were her favorite. He would sometimes write her poems and read them to her like he used to when they were courting.

It sometimes made him sad to be at home. It was where her absence was most keenly felt because it was the place she was supposed to be. Everything reminded him of her – her clothes in the closet, her bonnet on the dresser, and the statues in the gardens that they had picked out together.

One summer morning as the birds tweeted outside his window, he decided to pay Elizabeth a visit at the cemetery to talk to her about possibly selling his home in Cincinnati. As he sat on the stone steps, he said,

"I don't know if I should stay here. It's so quiet in the house without you. I'm thinking maybe I should pack up our belongings and head east. I miss you so much."

He wiped a tear from his eye.

"I walked by a school on the way here. There were children outside playing, boys pulling little girls' pigtails and girls swinging and singing 'Mary Had a Little Lamb.' I thought of our desire for a family. Would it break your heart if I looked for another? I'll never find a woman that could replace you. But, still, the house is so quiet, so terribly quiet."

He listened to the wind whistle in the trees. He couldn't feel her presence and he wasn't sure if he had an answer. He decided to give it more time. After all, he had a life here. If the feeling remained for a few more months, he would seek employment elsewhere, perhaps in the south. He had several friends in Louisiana he could write to and a brother in Missouri. He decided the best course of action was to throw himself into his work.

Things got back to normal at Hoffner and Clark. Jacob gave Matthew a vacation and took over for a couple of weeks. Work gave him a sense of purpose and he enjoyed socializing with customers and clients. Pork and whiskey sales were up and more requests came in every day from New Orleans and St. Louis. With each passing day, the pain began to subside. He stayed late hours at the office, not liking to go home to an empty house and invited more friends over in the evening to keep him company.

Henry was a frequent houseguest and they enjoyed reminiscing about their time in England. In their youth, they had caused quite a ruckus at the pubs and often woke in a boarding house not remembering what had transpired the night before. They had traveled to Stonehenge, visited Buckingham Palace, and enjoyed their share of fish and chips.

Henry begged Jacob to return with him to England. Jacob felt he wasn't up for a journey quite yet. It didn't feel right to be so far from Elizabeth's grave, he felt somehow her spirit was tied to her grave along with her body. He tried to explain this to Henry, but Henry would simply laugh and tell Jacob to pour another shot of whiskey and live a little. This went on for a few weeks, until Jacob realized his work was suffering from all the late nights with Henry. So, he sent his friend on his way and promised to meet him in England in the New Year.

Jacob resumed his duties at the Masonic lodge. The men looked up to him, Jacob being one of the oldest members of the group. He was something of a mentor to the younger men. The camaraderie of the men made the nights less lonely. The recitation of the rituals gave him a sense of order and routine. He felt renewed by their mission to better the community. Masons were called to improve the world beyond just themselves. It was their calling to better the places in which they lived. They built a new school playground, donated funds to an asylum for the mentally ill and funded several church activities. Often the lodge was rented out to groups for free for plays, meetings or fundraisers.

Jacob had profited greatly through his business dealings, had no one to care for but himself and felt it his duty to share in his wealth. He often hosted fundraisers for groups himself, enjoying the planning and preparations for the events. Living so close, people would often trickle over to his house afterward. He felt like he knew almost everyone in town.

The months passed in this fashion and Jacob began to feel like himself again. His visits to Elizabeth had decreased as his socializing increased. He no longer desired to move, but was content to solidify his place in the community.

Every once in a while, he would see a pretty woman at a fundraiser who would give him a smile, but, then her husband would come up and put his arm around her waist. All of the pretty ones seemed to already be married, so Jacob resigned himself to the single life. He was in his forties, and his desires were not nearly as urgent as they had been in his youth. But, being human, he would look around. Most of the women looked overwhelmed by responsibility or were done up in lace, corsets and powder looking like they had never lifted a finger aside from ringing for a servant. Very few reminded him of Elizabeth with her beauty, but also her sense of caring and compassion. Of course, very few women had husbands as nurturing and caring as Jacob.

One particular woman named Helen would often stare at him with her sad eyes. She was the wife of Wayne Gehringer, the other Master Mason in the Order.

Wayne was not a humble man, he was a rough man who seemed more interested in the power and control inherent in his position than the lodge's mission to better the community. He noticed Helen gazing at Jacob with his grey eyes and dashing black cape. Wayne pulled Helen closer and walked away brusquely. Wayne was not fond of Jacob. It was widely acknowledged that when the Grandmaster passed, Jacob was expected to take over the Order. But, Wayne had other plans. Wayne wasn't going to let the do-gooder widower take his coveted place. It was rumored that Wayne knocked Helen about and that was the cause of her sad eyes.

Jacob tried to be kind to Wayne, offering to collaborate with him on projects and inviting him to fundraiser after parties. But Wayne would have none of it, often not inviting him to committee meetings because it "slipped his mind" or outright suggesting that Jacob's ideas were too grand for the Order and they should be focusing on smaller concerns like fish fries and picnics rather than building schools and churches.

When Jacob went home that night, he felt sorry for poor Helen. She shouldn't have to spend her days in fear of a man like Wayne. She was so beautiful and looked so sad. He told himself his feelings were noble and entirely out of concern. But, he wondered if his feelings were really more about jealousy. Wayne and Helen had four children, all living, and here was Jacob, all alone, with only his journal to keep him company in the lamplight.

9

As Anna pulled up to the sawhorses, it almost didn't feel like she was in a graveyard. The sun shone brightly overhead and all around the grounds were showing signs of life. The daffodils were starting to bloom. The new grass was sprouting up through the shards of winter brown. She walked slowly, nervously toward the gravesite, afraid that the ghost might jump out from around a corner and spook her. She walked around the female statue down to the steps and sat down. She felt in her pocket for the key and pulled it out. "Journey" she read again. What did it mean?

"I'm back. I did what you asked," she called out.

She listened, but heard only birds in the trees.

"I found the key. Is this what you wanted to leave me? What does it mean?"

She sat down, but heard no answer. She started to rise and walk back to the car, but she felt a heat along her shoulder blades. She looked behind her and saw the kind, grey eyes. Jacob was sitting on the steps, his cane brushing the step in front of her and his hand on her shoulder.

"I want you to go on a journey," he said with a smile.

"To where?" she asked.

"Journey of the mind, the heart, the soul, Indiana," said Jacob.

"Indiana? What's in Indiana?" said Anna.

"Have you ever heard of Parke County, Indiana?" Jacob asked.

"Isn't that where they have all of the old covered bridges?" Anna asked.

"Yes, in my day – they weren't old. They were in peak condition. But, yes, that is what I'm referring to."

He proceeded to tell her that beneath one particular bridge, Jackson Bridge, near Bloomingdale, he had hidden something behind a brick underneath the bridge.

"But, what is it? What did you hide there?" she asked.

"It wouldn't be much of a journey, an adventure, if I told you now. I guess you're just going to have to go and see for yourself," he winked at her.

And just like that, he was gone.

This is madness, Anna thought.

Why was she here? Running errands for a ghost? She picked up the key and set it down on the step.

I should just leave it here, she thought.

What's he going to do? Follow me? Haunt me?

She picked it up again. There was no going back, she realized. She wanted to complain about it, it was her nature. She wanted to fuss and whine and do nothing. But, there was a fire in her belly.

She felt the heaviness of the key in her hands. It grounded her. She was about to go on an adventure, she thought. She smiled and skipped up the stairs.

"See you soon," she called out to the air. She pulled out her cell phone, 5:00, where had the day gone? She broke into a jog.

As she got to her car, her cell phone rang.

"Where have you been?" asked Patrick. "I thought you got off work around noon," he said.

"I decided to go to yoga class," said Anna.

"Really?" said Patrick incredulously. "Good for you.

Where are you now?" he asked.

"I'm on my way home. I should be there in about 20 minutes," she said.

"Great. Are you up for going out tonight? Some of the actors from the show invited us out to dinner," said Patrick.

"Sure. I'll shower and change when I get home. See you soon," said Anna.

"I love you," said Patrick.

"I love you too," said Anna and clicked "end call."

As Anna drove home, she thought about how nice it was of Patrick to invite her out to meet his new friends. He didn't often do that. But, she wasn't looking forward to it. He was in his own little theater world with his theater friends and being around them only made her feel more like an outsider. She doubted anyone would even speak to her all evening. Maybe that was for the best tonight, then she wouldn't have to answer a bunch of questions about her day.

She stopped to get the mail out of the lockbox in the hallway and then turned the key to the apartment. She could hear the shower running as she walked in, so she walked to the bedroom, opened the closet door and searched for something to wear. She settled upon a lightweight, blue crewneck sweater, a pair of skinny jeans and ballet flats. As she finished pulling the sweater over her head, she heard the shower turn off.

"Anna, is that you?" Patrick called out.

"No, it's the ghost of Christmas Past," Anna responded.

She ran over to her laptop and quickly searched Google Maps for directions to Bloomingdale, Indiana – 3 hour drive. She was going to have to ask off work.

Patrick emerged from the bathroom wearing black jeans and a hunter green Henley shirt which made his eyes look even greener. He was such a handsome man, Anna thought, wishing she could feel something more than physical attraction for him.

"You look nice," Patrick said approvingly. "There's something about you today. You seem happier for some reason," he said.

"I am. I think it must be the yoga," Anna replied.

"Maybe you could try a few more yoga positions tonight," Patrick said pulling her into his arms and kissing her while running his fingers down her back.

"Quit. We're going to be late," Anna said pulling away.

"O.K. But, the offer's on the table," Patrick said.

She grabbed his hand and pulled him out the front door. He opened the door to his black Chevy Camaro and she hopped in.

They made their way to Puccini's, an Italian Bistro a few blocks from their home. Seated at a booth in the far corner, two girls waved at Patrick and motioned for them to come over.

"You didn't tell me they were all girls." Anna whispered as she plastered on a fake smile and walked over to the table.

"Hi Patrick! Is this your girlfriend? Nice to meet you. My name's Ashley," the slim brunette said and shook Anna's hand.

"Hi. I'm Megan," said a prettier version of Anna with a slight wave of her hand.

They sat down and Anna busied herself examining the menu like she was studying for a chemistry exam. The girls excitedly talked about the play, giggling and lightly touching Patrick on the hand.

"What do you do?" Megan said. "Are you an actress, too?" she said turning to Anna.

"No, I work at the FedEx warehouse," Anna said.

"She's a writer, too. She likes to write. Right, honey?" Patrick said.

"Yeah, it's just sort of a hobby, though," Anna said looking down.

As they continued to talk, Anna checked the girls out. Ashley looked to be about 22, was tall and thin with long brown hair and was very bubbly and animated. Megan looked slightly younger, maybe 20, was petite, blonde, wearing a retro pinup girl dress that flared at the bottom and a cardigan. She had full Angelina Jolie lips. Anna looked down at her crewneck sweater and jeans and felt wracked with insecurity.

Why did she even care?

But, she could see the way his eyes sparkled when they talked and she felt the pangs of jealousy, nonetheless. The food arrived and Anna watched them daintily eat their grilled chicken salads.

Who orders salad at Puccini's? Anna thought.

Anna savored her cheese ravioli with marinara sauce and asked for a bite of Patrick's pizza. Patrick talked mainly to his castmates, full of excitement about *Love's Glory*, the show they were all performing in the end of May. Anna said little and tried to send Patrick telepathic messages that she was ready to go. When the waitress came, Anna asked for the check. Patrick continued talking.

"Yeah, Jonathan has it out for me, man. I better get those lines down," Patrick said.

What was he talking about? She must have zoned out. She didn't even know who Jonathan was. Patrick noticed Anna slipping on her jacket and putting her canvas shoulder bag over her arm.

"You ready to go?" asked Patrick.

"Yeah, I have work tomorrow. It was nice meeting you all," Anna said and scooted across the booth in an attempt to get Patrick to stand up. Ashley frowned, Megan sighed.

"You too," they said at the same time.

"I guess we'll need to practice our big romance scene tomorrow. Huh, Patrick?" Ashley said brazenly.

Patrick turned red, "I guess so," he said, standing up. Ashley stood up and hugged him.

"See you tomorrow," she said to Patrick.

They were silent the entire car ride home. When they walked in, Patrick grabbed Anna from behind and put his arms around her waist.

"You're not jealous of those girls? Are you?" he asked.

"No, of course not. Have fun with your big love scene tomorrow," Anna said sarcastically.

"Maybe you should help me practice," Patrick said, pulling her crewneck sweater over her head.

Anna acquiesced to his advances. The evening had triggered her feelings of inadequacy and sex was a nice distraction from her self-loathing. Patrick led her to the bed and she surrendered. Thirty minutes later, they were asleep.

When she woke, she had nearly forgotten all about her ghost mission. She leaned over to pull the cord on the lamp on the nightstand and found a note from Patrick.

"Thanks for the practice. I should do great today," it read. She thought of that Ashley girl and snarled. She pushed her face into the pillow, the short lived passion of the night before seemed far away. The morning light illuminated all the flaws in their partnership and reminded her of her dissatisfaction with her life.

She glanced over and looked at the time. 20 minutes to get ready for work. She sat up and robotically went through the motions of getting ready. While brushing her teeth, she remembered her task for the morning. She needed to ask Brad if she could have the next day off so she could venture out to Parke County. Brad wasn't going to be pleased. She needed to think up an excuse. She thought hard the entire drive in and finally settled on a good one.

When she arrived, Midge was pulling into her parking spot at the same time in her yellow Volkswagen Beetle.

"Hey girlie," she said to Anna as she pulled out a plastic shopping bag full of snacks out of the backseat.

"Good morning, Midge," Anna said.

"You're looking a little worse for wear this morning," said Midge.

"Late night," said Anna.

As they walked in together, Anna filled her in on Ashley and Megan and Anna's attempts to seduce Patrick out of finding them attractive.

"You need to let that boy go," said Midge. "I had an ex-husband like him; first they're winking and smiling at the young girls. The next thing you know, those girls are in your living room with their panties on your coffee table," said Midge.

"I don't think he's actually doing anything with them," Anna said. "I'm just being paranoid and insecure," she said.

"Well, you don't need it, pretty girl like you. You need to find someone that doesn't go around kissing other girls as part of his career plan. Actors – they're just trouble waiting to happen," said Midge.

Anna processed the advice and made her way to her post. Brad was switching on the conveyor belt to start the line going for the day. As he walked past, Anna quickly blurted out,

"Brad, can I talk to you on break? I need tomorrow off."

"You better have a good reason," Brad said. "I don't know if I can get someone else to cover you on that short of notice."

Anna nodded and filled the first box down the line with the ream of paper. The day passed like all the others, music in the background, box, paper, box, paper.

At break, she found Brad in his office, drinking coffee and checking sports scores on the internet. She knocked softly and he looked up, mildly annoyed.

"Oh hey, what's up?" Brad said.

"Tomorrow, my mom is having knee surgery and she needs me to drive her home from the hospital. I would have given you more notice, but my mom thought my sister, Alyce, was going to drive her, but Alyce's daughter has the flu. Is it O.K.?" she asked.

Brad said, "Fine. But, don't make a habit of it, Perrault."

Anna nodded and walked to the break room with a little skip in her step. It wasn't entirely a lie. Her mom was having knee surgery the next day. But, she and Anna had never been close and Anna's more dutiful sister, Alyce, was in fact driving her mom to the appointment. Their father died when she was 10 and Alyce was 12. Her mother clung to her older auburn-haired sister, instead of flaxen Anna who reminded her too much of Anna's father, Dennis. Alyce, being very girly and popular, never quite understood Anna with her tomboy clothes, quiet demeanor and propensity for holing up in a corner to write. They rarely talked. But, boy, did they come in handy today. Anna couldn't wait to get home and start planning.

Three hours later, she was on the couch in a t-shirt and sweats, her laptop perched on top of her knees. She had printed out directions to Jackson Bridge, found a cute diner online for lunch, and checked out some parks in the area. Tomorrow was supposed to be unusually warm, she would only need a light jacket if she needed one at all and she thought maybe a short hike through the woods sounded like fun. By the time Patrick arrived home for dinner, she had packed, cleaned up the house and was surfing Facebook.

She heard the rattle of Patrick's keys as he opened the front door.

"What's got into you? Yoga? Cleaning? What happened to the Anna we all know and love?" he joked.

The Anna we all know and love? She rolled her eyes. *He loved depression on a stick, in sweatpants next to a coffee table full of crumbs? Yeah, right.*

"How was rehearsal?" she asked.

"Great. I think me and Ashley really nailed it today,"

he said as he walked in the bedroom to change.

I bet you did, she thought.

"What's new on Facebook?" Patrick asked.

"Oh you know, same old, same old, people posting funny videos of their kids and pictures of their dinner," Anna replied.

Patrick sat on the couch next to her and flipped on the TV.

"How was work?" he asked.

"Fine," she replied and pretended to be engrossed in *Wheel of Fortune.*

She decided not to tell him about taking off the next day. He would want to skip rehearsal and come with her. Better for him to just think she was at work.

"Want some tuna casserole? It should be ready in about ten minutes," Anna said.

Patrick smiled and said, "That sounds good."

They ate dinner, and watched several hours of TV. Patrick said he was tired and went off to bed. Anna stayed up watching late night talk shows and fell asleep on the couch.

The next morning, shortly after Patrick kissed her on the forehead and told her to get ready for work, he was out the door and the day was hers.

Anna threw on her navy jacket, grabbed her directions off of the printer, picked her purse up off of the floor and headed to the car.

The drive was long, but pleasurable. Traffic wasn't very heavy and she sang to herself as she passed semis and minivans to get into the fast lane. She arrived in Parke County around noon, and set her GPS to find the diner she saw online – the Thirty-Six Saloon and Family Restaurant. She liked the old saloon look of it and was eager to try the chicken salad. As she entered the rustic doors, she noticed the abundance of taxidermy lining the walls – grizzly bears, badgers, and a moose. She was in the country all right.

This was a far cry from any restaurant she had visited in Cincinnati. The atmosphere seemed straight out of Eastern Kentucky. She noticed some local men in cowboy hats at the bar enjoying their afternoon beer. Hazy cigarette smoke wafted through the dining area. Anna decided she might enjoy sitting outside instead and walked out the rear doors to the outdoor patio. She sat at a table near the railing, and pressed down on the plastic gingham tablecloth to keep it from blowing in the wind. A young girl in a tank top and jeans came over to hand her a menu and take her drink order.

"I'll just have an iced tea," said Anna as she began to peruse the menu.

She had planned on chicken salad, but in this atmosphere, it seemed wrong to eat anything that didn't contain fat and salt, so she opted for cheese fries. Dipping the gooey fries into ketchup, she felt like she was actually having fun. She pulled her map out of her purse to figure out how far she was from Rockville Lake Park where she had decided to go hiking. From what she could tell, it should be no more than a 15 minute drive. Anna paid the waitress and continued on her way.

Parking near the lake, Anna got out and explored her surroundings. She found the marker for the nature trails and tromped off into the woods. The silence of nature felt like a warm cocoon. She couldn't fathom why Patrick would want to live in New York City, with all the noise and cars and inescapable people. This was the way to live, so quiet that it felt like God was watching you. She wondered what she would find under Jackson Bridge and why she had not gone there first. She reasoned that she wanted to drag out the excitement, her hike being a form of extended foreplay. Her everyday life was so mundane full of box, paper, Patrick droning on about backstage antics and nothing to look forward to.

But, today was just for her and it held hope, if not promise. Maybe it would be money or jewelry or some rare antique. She could see the clearing in the trees and knew the trail was coming to an end. She was starting to regret the cheese fries as her stomach began to gurgle and fuss. She thought about calling her mother to check in on her after her surgery, but decided against it. She was sure it was uneventful and her mother would want to talk for an hour and Anna wanted to get to the bridge before 2:00.

She got in the car and turned on the GPS. The signal wasn't strong in this part of the country and she hoped she would be able to find it. The road became narrower and started to wind through the trees. She saw the white painted structure resembling the photo she had seen on the internet just ahead. She looked for a gravel turnoff in the road and parked the car.

She got out and walked toward the bridge. The white paint was chipping and the red paint with the words "Jackson Bridge" was barely legible. Jacob had said there would be a loose brick underneath the bridge. She felt for the key in her jacket pocket and walked toward the embankment. A bubbling creek flowed under the bridge and Anna slipped on some wet mud on her way down the hill. It was dank and musty under the bridge and several young lovers had carved their names in the brick. She examined the old brick looking for any crack in the cement. All of the ones near the top looked fairly intact. She panicked, wondering if someone had found the loose brick and patched it back up. She crouched down on her knees to feel along the bricks at the bottom. The second to last brick jostled when her fingers brushed it. She crammed her fingers in the hole and tugged. It wouldn't budge.

She pounded on the ground in frustration. She got up and went back to the car looking for anything she could use as a tool. Opening the trunk, she found the car jack that she had never used and thought that might work. She trudged back down the hill and shoved the jack in the tiny corner of rock. It took nearly an hour but little by little she dislodged the old brick and set it on the ground. She reached her tiny hand into the wet crevice and felt something metal inside. She grabbed the corner of it and pulled it out. Another box with another inscription!

It read, "The only journey is the journey within."

She pulled the key out of her pocket. There was a small key hole in the front of the box. She turned the key and the top popped open revealing a small leather bound journal. Slightly disappointed it wasn't money; she ran her fingers over the old brown leather and sat on the muddy ground to open it. The front page was yellow and the writing a bit faint, but it read "Diary of Jacob Hoffner." She flipped through the pages; there were nearly 300 pages of handwriting. She smiled at her discovery, placed the metal box back inside the foundation of the bridge and pushed the brick back in as best she could.

Climbing up the hillside, she felt a little out of breath and decided she clearly needed more exercise. She wanted to sit down and read it right then and there. But it was close to 3:00 and she wanted to get home at her usual time so Patrick wouldn't suspect anything was amiss.

Driving home, she began to feel like she had made a friend, a friend with whom she shared a secret. This made her happy, even if the friend happened to be a ghost that died 100 years ago. She looked forward to reading the diary and wondered if it contained important information that Jacob wanted her to know.

When she got back, she was surprised to find that Patrick wasn't home. That was odd, as he was almost always home by 6:00. She flipped open her laptop and checked her email. No messages. She checked her phone and there was nothing. Exhausted, she threw her things in the corner, hid the diary in her nightstand under some pads of paper and flopped down on the couch.

A couple of hours later, she woke from a nap and strange dreams about falling into water. Her phone was on the coffee table and she noticed there was a message waiting. Patrick had called to say he was going out with friends from the show and would be home late.

Anna went into the kitchen, made herself a peanut butter sandwich, grabbed a bag of potato chips and a Coke and sat back on the couch to devour her dinner. She flipped on the TV but saw nothing but reruns. Her curiosity got the better of her and she went to fetch the diary. The ornate, cursive handwriting was hard to make out, but she squinted her eyes and slowly got used to the flow of it.

It began with Jacob's moment on the bridge when he wasn't sure whether he wanted to live or die. She had been there, more than once. She pictured him sitting there in the place she had just been and felt instant kinship with his pain and depressed soul.

She read about his struggles with letting go of his dead wife and his strong desire for a child of his own. Anna herself wasn't sure if she wanted children. She didn't feel like she was capable of caring for herself much less another small being. But the pages depicted Jacob as a kind, sensitive caring soul and she no longer worried that she was influenced by a malevolent spirit.

She was just starting to get into Jacob's involvement with the Masons when she heard footsteps on the apartment building stairs. She flung the diary under the couch and turned on the TV. The 11:00 clock news was on. Patrick stumbled in the door, disheveled and a little drunk.

"Hey Anna, what's up? Miss me?" He slumped next to her reeking of bourbon and cigarettes.

He leaned over to kiss her and she turned her head.

"Ooh, you smell disgusting. Why don't you take a shower first before you go crawling all up on me?" she said.

Patrick looked disappointed and muttered "alright."

She lay back down on the couch and pretended to be asleep. She had no desire to be his drunken plaything tonight. She wished he would go. She wished he was gone. She wished she was free.

10

One sweltering evening in August, as Jacob was locking up the store, a postman came running up to him as he turned to leave.

"Wait, sir. Mr. Hoffner, sir," said the postman.

Jacob recognized the pimply-faced boy named Billie who brought the daily post.

"Yes, Billie? What can I do for you?" said Jacob.

"There's a telegram for you sir. It's marked 'urgent'," he said handing him an envelope.

Jacob thanked the boy and stood in the street ripping off the top of the envelope. It read, "Sarah has passed. Tuberculosis. Molly an orphan, staying with neighbors. Please advise."

Jacob was stunned. He thought that Sarah looked a bit under the weather when he visited, but had no idea it was so serious.

Molly an orphan? That poor beautiful cherub. She must be so frightened. She had not a soul in the world.

Then and there, he resolved that he would take care of her. He sent word in the morning asking if the neighbor could bring her to Cincinnati and gave his address.

The morning she arrived she was dressed in her best

dress, hair pulled back in barrettes, clutching a stuffed blue bunny and holding a tiny suitcase. At first she was timid, but after a few minutes, she flung her tiny arms around his neck, and he picked her up. He thanked the neighbor for taking such good care of her and offered to pay her travel expenses. The neighbor, Lucinda, said it had been no bother, but that the girl had been found crying on the front porch after her mother had been dead for several hours.

Jacob showed the little girl up to a room he had fixed up for her, complete with a rocking horse and a child size bed with a pink quilt and lace dust ruffle. She paced about the room for a time, feeling alien in the new household and then quietly sat down and started playing with the new dollhouse he had purchased. He left her alone and went to make her a bit to eat.

A few minutes later, she emerged from the room, walked down to the kitchen to see what he was doing and asked to see the rest of the grounds. He showed her the Italian sculptures, the pond, the greenhouses and the garden, the hedges, the roses – all the plants and statuary that Elizabeth so dearly loved. Molly liked the animal sculptures the best and asked to sit on the lions. He lifted her up to sit on the mighty beast's back.

"Roar!" she said and giggled.

Within a few weeks, Molly fit right into Jacob's routine. He walked her to school in the morning before he went to work, he hired a neighbor girl to watch her after school until he returned home, and every night they read books before bed. She filled his life with joy and he was grateful for her company.

One evening when he walked in the door, Molly ran toward him holding a pair of sparkly wings.

"Uncle Jacob! Uncle Jacob! I'm in a play!" she said.

"You are? Well, what play are you in, little darling?" he said.

"A Midsummer Night's Dream!" she squealed. "I'm a

fairy!" She danced around the room with her wings. "See how they sparkle, Uncle Jacob?" she said.

He told her she would be the prettiest fairy in the whole class.

After Molly had drifted off to sleep, Jacob sat up reading *Walden*, a new book by a man named Henry David Thoreau. Jacob's mind skimmed through several pages until he came upon a line that stood out to him, "I know of no more encouraging fact than the unquestionable ability of man to elevate his life by a conscious endeavor." He thought about that for a moment and wondered about the ways in which he could elevate his life.

He began to think about other poor children like Molly who had been orphaned and had no wealthy relative to take them in and care for them. He felt very passionately that those children should receive proper care. At the next meeting of Masonic Lodge 234, Jacob decided he would make a motion that their yearly project should be to build an orphanage. There was an order of nuns who had been trying to get a new one built and they had over 100 children under their charge. They simply needed the funding. Jacob would offer to pay half the cost himself.

At last Jacob had a sense of purpose. He closed the book and slept well that night. He dreamed of dancing fairies and smiling orphans. He knew in his heart that this was what he was meant to do in this world. The next Masonic meeting was in two days on Thursday night, he would bring it up for a vote then.

The next evening, Molly had play practice at Sugar Valley Elementary School. She was so excited she was jumping up and down when he arrived home from work and dragging him out the door to the wagon before he could sit down.

The parents were all filtering into the school auditorium. Punch and cookies were set out and the parents milled around the table as their vivacious youngsters took the stage. The schoolteacher, Mrs.

Hammerle, was trying to settle the chaotic group down and usher them backstage to try on costumes. As Jacob reached for the ladle to the punch bowl, Jacob noticed Helen, Wayne's wife, picking up a chocolate chip cookie from the bowl on the table.

"Why hello, Mrs. Gehringer. How are you this evening?" Jacob asked.

She smiled and said, "I'm just fine, Mr. Hoffner. Is your little girl in the play?"

"Why yes, the little lass is playing a fairy. Which one of your little ones is in the show?" he asked.

"My oldest, William is playing the donkey," she replied.

"Oh, the boy's an ass, is he?" Jacob chuckled and pulled out a chair for Helen to sit down.

"Indeed, sometimes he can be," she said. "Takes after his father that one," she said with her smile turning downward.

She wrung her hands and looked down at her lap. Jacob wasn't quite sure what to say. He didn't wish to badmouth her husband in front of her, but could see the pain in her expression.

"The donkey learns his lesson in the end, doesn't he? Isn't that how the story goes? It's been so long since I read any Shakespeare," Jacob said.

"I don't recall. I guess we'll have to watch the show and find out," she said turning her attention to the stage, shutting down further communication.

Just then, the children came out on stage, scripts in hand that were handwritten by Ms. Hammerle. The children were too young to master Shakespeare's words so she had written an elementary version of the play herself. The little fairies flitted across the stage on their tiptoes.

Jacob leaned over to Helen, "Aren't they adorable?" he said.

She didn't reply. It seemed she felt she had already been disloyal to her husband by speaking with him. Jacob felt bad, but his face lit up when Molly appeared onstage. She curtsied, spun around, tripped and then popped up with a smile. It was beyond cute.

When rehearsal ended, Jacob gave Helen a slight wave, took Molly's tiny hand and walked her to the wagon. It was late and she had school the next day. The little cherub was yawning when they arrived home and more than ready for bed.

Jacob thought about Helen and thought about Wayne. He wasn't sure what to do about that situation. It seemed best just to stay out of it. But, he felt like Helen needed his help.

Maybe he would try and talk to Wayne at the meeting tomorrow night. He could try and gain Wayne's support for the orphanage. Maybe if Wayne was involved in a project, there would less time for him to be at home terrorizing Helen. Jacob was a peaceful man and didn't like to stir up conflict. But, he had a feeling Wayne needed to be reminded of what being a Mason was supposed to be all about.

11

"Where's the aspirin?" Patrick groaned. He reached into the refrigerator for a bottle of water trying to hydrate his hangover.

"It's in the medicine cabinet on the top shelf," Anna responded.

"Oh, my head. Liquor before beer, never fear. Beer before liquor, never sicker. Why don't I listen?" Patrick said turning on the shower.

As he closed the bathroom door, Anna felt annoyed. His presence was beginning to feel claustrophobic.

"I should just break up with him," she thought.

But then, she looked around the apartment at all of her furniture and clothes and it all seemed like more than she could deal with at the moment. She needed time to figure this whole thing out and decide what to do.

By the time Patrick got out of the shower, she was dressed and ready for work.

"Hey Patrick, I might be home late tonight, O.K.?" she said.

"Really? How come?" said Patrick.

"I'm going to head to the library after work, do some research. I'm thinking about writing a book" she said.

"That's great. I'll probably be at rehearsal late anyway. Give me a call if you want me to save you some dinner," he said.

She gave him a quick peck on the lips and headed out the door, the journal hidden inside her purse. The work day passed slowly as usual. Midge was complaining about her arthritic knee and bragging about her grandson making honor roll. Brad was his usual charming self. He seemed to work her twice as hard, continually questioning her about her mother's surgery and acting like he was some kind of saint for giving her the day off.

When she clocked out, she hugged Midge and made her way to the car in the setting sun. She stopped by McDonald's to grab a burger and a Coke and then drove down Hwy 68 toward the county library. As she passed the old church where Patrick's community theater group performed, she saw Patrick's car in the parking lot. On an impulse, she decided to stop by quickly and let him know that she would likely not be home until very late. That way he wouldn't be calling asking what time she would be home.

She walked up the concrete steps and opened the heavy double doors, that girl Megan who she had met the other night was stage right delivering a soliloquy to the audience about the hardships of war. When she finished, the director, who was sitting in the pews, gave her some notes about "feeling the pain" of the time period. Anna felt somewhat bemused by the exasperated look on the girl's face as she explained that she was trying to feel the pain but she had no personal trauma to draw on. The director rolled his eyes at her and whispered to the assistant director sitting next to him.

Anna scanned the room looking for Patrick and caught a glimpse of him behind the curtain on the left side of the stage. Ashley, the brunette from dinner, was giggling and whispering in his ear. Patrick had a huge smile on his face and was stroking the small of her back.

Screw him, Anna thought. *He can just wonder where I am when I don't come home tonight.*

Then she slipped away unseen back out the heavy church doors into the darkening night air.

When she arrived at the library, the clerks were starting to shut down computers and tidy up the workstations. They were closing in one hour. Anna quickly made her way over to her favorite spot, a comfy chair at the end of the reference section. Patrons rarely walked back that way so it was a comfy spot to sit and peruse books. She pulled the old journal out of her bag and began to read.

She read about Jacob's trips to Europe, his love of horticulture, his love of beauty and his compassion for his young niece, Molly. Anna had always wanted to travel abroad, but Patrick was always in a show and there was never a good time for them to get away. She began to fantasize about what it would be like to go there by herself, how much she would need to save, and what she would do if she ever got to go to London.

She was just getting to the part about Jacob's plans for building an orphanage when a plump, grey haired woman with glasses informed her that the library would be closing in ten minutes. Anna looked at the journal; she was only a third of the way through it and eager to finish it.

She wondered where to go next. She didn't want to go home. She felt angry at Patrick for flirting with this size 2 girl that was the polar opposite of Anna. It made her seethe inside. But at the same time she wasn't up for the fight. She didn't feel strong enough. She just wanted to avoid him and hope the problems went away.

She was starting to feel wild and like taking some risks. If Jacob could visit Europe in the 1800s, what the hell was she doing on a Friday night? She decided to go out dancing. She hadn't been dancing since she was in her early twenties. Yes, a night of dancing and drinking. After all she had been through this week, she felt she deserved it.

Anna looked down at her clothing. She was still in her khakis and t-shirt from work. She went out to the car to see if she had anything suitable to wear to a club. She opened the trunk and rummaged through a pile of laundry until she found a black tank top and a pair of jeans. She slipped back into the library to change and walked out the doors as they were locking up and turning out the lights.

The Red Zone was a club on the north end of town that she used to frequent in her crazy college days. It was in an abandoned old warehouse in a sketchy part of town. She was a little nervous her car might get broken into when she parked. From the exterior, it was hard to tell that there was a club at all. But, she could see the flashing red lights through the dusty windows. She walked to the front door and got out her ID for the bouncer. To her surprise, it was the same guy that had worked there years ago. His name was Stuart. He always wore a black leather jacket and had a Mohawk with a tinge of red in it.

"Hey Stuart, remember me?" she said.

"Oh my God! How have you been?" he exclaimed.

Anna had been a regular party girl in her twenties. He shone the flashlight on her ID, charged her the $5 cover and she walked inside. The thump, thump, thump of the club music intoxicated her and she got swept up in it. She made her way through the crowd of people to the back bar and ordered an amaretto sour with extra cherries. As she sipped the sweet liquor, she surveyed the room. Mostly college students in hipster clothing gyrated and twisted to the dance music. A few aging Goths in black leather with shaved heads bopped along with them. She found it a little sad. But, she was about to dive in right along with them. Anna set her empty drink down on the bar and began to sway to the music. It felt so freeing, so alive. She danced for hours, arms swaying over her head, hips moving from side to side.

Around midnight, she was drunk, every couple of songs, she would go refill her drink. When she went back out on the dance floor after her third refill, she felt a man's hips behind her grinding her backside along to the music. She looked behind her and saw a very handsome, very drunk blonde guy who looked to be about 25. His t-shirt was stained with sweat and his eyes weren't focusing. But the heat of his hips felt so good next to hers. She turned around and wrapped her arms around his neck. He began to kiss her, and she felt the heat rise in her chest. A few minutes later, he had her outside behind the building, pressed up against the brick wall. He unzipped her jeans and inserted himself into her. Their mutual breathing rose and fell in a burst of passion. Within minutes, he was finished, her pants were zipped and he was between two cars throwing up. When she went back inside, he was nowhere to be found. She continued to drink and dance to the music, not thinking - just enjoying the movement. By the time the club closed down at 4:00 a.m. she was drunk, sore and out of breath.

She was happy that the drive home wasn't long and there weren't many cars on the road. She stumbled up the apartment steps, dropping her keys halfway up and then fumbling with the lock. To her surprise, Patrick was still awake and sitting on the couch watching a late night movie.

"Where the hell have you been?" he asked.

"I decided to go dancing," she replied.

"You couldn't call me? I called you about 10 times, left messages," he said.

"Well, I couldn't hear my phone in the club," she replied.

"Unbelievable. I was worried sick. You could have at least called me," he said.

"Sorry," Anna slurred. "I wasn't aware that you owned me," she replied.

"Do you love me? You rarely say it anymore. You push me away when I try to kiss you. What the hell is going on with you?" he screamed coming toward her.

"I'm sorry, O.K. I got done at the library, and I thought it might be fun to go out. I didn't figure you'd miss me. I saw you at rehearsal with your arm around Ashley. What do you care?" she spat back at him.

"We're in a play together. It's my job. At least she looks at me when I talk to her. Look at you. You look like some overgrown teenager. When are you going to grow up? You blame everyone else for your problems while you stay in your dead end job that you hate. I'm not the problem, Anna, you are!" he yelled.

Then he turned around, went into the bedroom and slammed the door. Anna sat down on the couch in stunned silence. The words burned because she could feel some truth in them. She walked into the bathroom, splashed water on her face and picked up her pajamas that were still strewn upon the floor from that morning. She stared a hole into the bedroom door, trying to think of a comeback so she could go in there and rage into his face. But, instead she clumsily made her way to the couch and laid down. Within minutes, she passed out.

The next morning felt sobering in more ways than one. Anna and Patrick didn't speak. He quietly ate his cereal and left without a word. Anna called in to work, complaining of the stomach flu to Brad. He did not sound pleased, and she was sure she would pay for this later. Her head was throbbing and she went back to sleep on the couch for several more hours. She slowly started to come back to life after eating a banana and taking half a bottle of Advil.

Patrick's words rang in her head. She was the problem. She was the one making herself miserable and refusing to change. She thought with shame of her actions the night before, her self-destructive desire to simply feel wanted and whole. The ache of her feelings of inadequacy seemed to overcome her. It felt true and yet, the last few days it had seemed like everything had changed. She had been full of curiosity, dreaming of exploration and adventure. It was all so confusing. She went and got the leather bound journal out of her car. *Why did Jacob leave this for her? It was just stories, stories about his life. What was the purpose?* She contemplated finishing the journal, but instead thought it best if she pay the cemetery another visit. She needed answers. She hadn't asked enough questions. She had gone on his little scavenger hunt and now wanted to know what it all meant. She felt that finding that out held the key to everything.

12

At half past six, Jacob left the office and made his way to the Masonic lodge. He was full of enthusiasm for his orphanage proposal. He had discussed it with Matthew that afternoon and Matthew thought it sounded like a terrific idea and something the Order should pursue. As he entered the lodge doors, he heard whispering and murmuring inside. The meeting wasn't supposed to start until 6:30, but several of the members were already present including Wayne Gehringer and three of his closest allies.

They looked up from their conversation.

"Hello, Jacob," said Cecil Bentley.

Jacob wondered what was going on and what they were talking about, but the group quickly dispersed and went to take their seats. As the meeting was called to order, the Grandmaster asked if there was any new business to be presented. As Jacob rose to speak, Wayne beat him to the punch and spoke first.

"I have been in discussion with the Presbyterian Church and they are in terrible need of new pews before Christmas. Some of the elder members of the congregation are very uncomfortable in the old ones.

Some have been removed and there isn't enough seating for the congregation. I propose that we use excess funds for the purchase of new pews."

There were several shouts of "Hear, hear," from his friends.

Jacob spoke next, "I have been in contact with the sisters of St. Francis. There are over 100 orphans in our community. They do not have adequate housing or education. The sisters have been doing what they can in the basement of an old building on Main St, but with the growing number of children whose parents have died from tuberculosis, cholera, factory accidents etc., they are in need of better facilities. I am willing to finance the building of a new orphanage providing half of the funds if the Order can provide the other half."

Wayne grunted and said, "Likely the children of thieves and prostitutes and other poor citizens of our community. Why should their young live lives of prosperity while fine, upstanding citizens of this community suffer? It is the state's job to take care of orphans, not ours. Just because you've chosen to care for one, doesn't mean it's the duty of this brotherhood. Many members of our Order attend the Presbyterian Church. There are not Catholics here. You, Jacob, don't even attend church, so I'm not sure what say you have in the matter. I veto Mr. Hoffner's proposal on the grounds that it is not in the best interest of the Order."

Jacob was stunned at this turn of events. He had not anticipated opposition and wasn't sure what to say.

As he struggled with a response, the Grandmaster said, "I think at our next meeting, we should put the two proposals to a vote, what say you?"

The members replied, "Aye."

The rest of the meeting was fairly routine, a new member was inducted and then the meeting adjourned for cocktails and socializing. Jacob found Matthew and asked his opinion of the meeting.

"Your idea is much better, Jacob. Wayne is causing a stir just to spite you. Maybe you should talk with him."

So, Jacob grabbed a glass of bourbon and wandered over to where Wayne stood fraternizing in a circle with three of the older members of the group.

He patted Wayne on the shoulder, "May I have a word?" he asked.

Wayne asked his friends if they would excuse him for a moment.

"I think we may have gotten off on the wrong foot," Jacob began. "I would like to invite you and your wife over for cocktails tomorrow evening," he said.

"I bet you would," said Wayne. "I heard you were chatting her up at the kid's school. Stay away from my wife, Hoffner."

Jacob replied, "I was just making conversation. I meant no offense. Just you – then? How about you come around tomorrow night and we have a chat, just you and me?"

Wayne looked at him with contempt, but acquiesced.

"I can be there at 8, you got whiskey?"

Jacob replied that he had several bottles of Kentucky's finest. Wayne nodded and turned back to his friends. Jacob wandered back to the buffet table filled with snacks and wondered what he had done wrong. Just then, Cecil Bentley walked over and whispered,

"I'd watch out for Gehringer if I were you. He's been spreading rumors that you're some kind of Satan worshiper because you don't attend church, says you're working for the devil to turn the Order in the wrong direction. He's even gone so far as to accuse you of coveting his wife. I wouldn't trust him, no matter what he says to you."

Cecil quietly walked away. Jacob took a minute to absorb this information. How could anyone believe that about him? It was preposterous. He needed to think long and hard about how to deal with a fellow like Wayne.

Jacob walked out into the cool night air, tightening his cape to block the chill wind. He felt he was in a predicament and needed to get some allies on his side. Wayne was beginning to make him feel like he was crazy. The false accusations burned in his mind. Did Wayne really believe them? Maybe he should stop speaking with Helen. If Elizabeth were still alive, she would be shocked by this turn of events. Jacob turned down the cobblestone path and walked the short distance to his house. When he arrived, Molly was already asleep. He walked into her bedroom, tucked her doll under her little arm and kissed her forehead. He had to protect his reputation for her sake. What if the rumors started at school? He closed her door and went off to bed, weary and sad.

The next day was Saturday and a day off from work. Jacob decided to take Molly to the newly erected Findlay Market. He was able to grow a great deal of produce in his own garden. But in the fall months, the Market offered an array of fruits and vegetables he wasn't able to grow on his own land. When he told Molly the news, she was very excited and put on her Sunday dress and a matching blue bonnet that Jacob had bought for her. She ran down the stairs begging Jacob to buy her some taffy when they got there.

"Only if you act like a lady and mind your manners," Jacob said.

"Oh I will, I will Papa."

Molly had fallen into the habit of calling Jacob Papa instead of Uncle Jacob. It made things easier and less confusing for her at school. And their relationship had become so close that she often forgot he wasn't her Papa.

The market was bustling with shoppers. A newsboy was shouting the latest news headlines on the street corner. Molly and Jacob slowly made their way from stand to stand, sampling apples and feeling tomatoes for ripeness. The smell of fish permeated the air. After much searching, they finally came upon a taffy maker and Molly cooed with delight watching the candy being pulled and prodded into shape. She stretched the sugary concoction between her tiny fingers and formed it into shapes.

"Look, Papa, I made a horse," she said.

"I see. Are you going to eat that horse, little lady?" he teased.

"Oh no," she said, reshaping it into a carrot, "I'm going to eat a carrot."

Jacob laughed. As they turned to walk away from the taffy stand, Jacob brushed shoulders with a family walking nearby.

"Oh, excuse me," Jacob said.

The woman turned around. It was Helen. Jacob noticed she had a black eye which was half swollen shut.

"Good God, what happened to you?" Jacob asked.

Helen looked down nervously, "I fell down the stairs. I'm so clumsy. I feel foolish going out in public like this, but we needed groceries."

Jacob knew that Helen had not fallen down the stairs. He felt anger rise in his chest.

"Can I help you with anything?" he asked.

"Oh no, I'm quite fine," she said. "I have the boys with me to help."

Jacob looked down at the four boys beside her carrying baskets.

"Well, good day to you," Jacob said.

Jacob tried to push the incident out of his mind for the remainder but his emotions were rising to a boil when Wayne arrived at his residence shortly after 8:00 p.m. Wayne strode in, threw his coat upon the sofa and requested a bourbon on the rocks.

"Now, what did you wish to talk about, Hoffner?" asked Wayne.

"I think the orphanage is much needed in this town, more so than some new church pews. You have children. Certainly if they were to lose you, you wouldn't want to see them suffer? I'm willing to foot more than half of the cost, and I would like your support in this matter."

Wayne tossed back his drink, "I'm an upstanding Christian man in this community, Hoffner. Several members of our church have supported the Masons and donated money to our fundraisers. They expect something in return. Now, these orphans aren't going to pay us back. It's like throwing money down a hole. I see no benefit in it. As for my own children, I have provisions set up for them should I die. That's what good parents do," said Wayne.

"But, not everyone has the means and family to do that. Isn't the Christian thing to do to provide for the poorest among us?" said Jacob.

"You have a very naïve view of the world, Hoffner. I've never liked you, flaunting your money about and keeping to your ways. You seem to think you can do anything you like. But, society has expectations, people have expectations and if you aren't on the offense, then you're going to be on the defense. If I were you, Hoffner, I'd withdraw your support for this orphanage idea and side with the church project, otherwise you just might find yourself on the defense," said Wayne.

"Like your wife with her bruised and bloodied face!" seethed Jacob. Wayne's face began to redden,

"I thought we were going to have a gentleman's meeting, but it seems you're rallying for a fight. I can do anything with my wife I damn well please, Hoffner. She's my property. You'd do well to remember that and mind your own business!" spat Wayne.

"You ought to be ashamed of yourself, spouting off at me about Christianity! You're no Christian. I may not be a churchgoing man, but I've read the Bible. And it says 'Love one another'. I don't think you even know what that means!" stormed Jacob rising to his feet.

"You're fighting a losing battle, Hoffner. I will take you down. How dare you speak to me that way. My father helped establish this town. I'm a Master Mason same as you and I have a lot of people on my side. When I'm Grandmaster I'll be making the decisions and my first order of business will be to oust you. So, I'd shut your goddamn mouth," screeched Wayne shaking his fist at Jacob.

"Get out of my house. I thought I could talk to you. But, there's no talking to you. You're a monster. People will see that. All they have to do is take one look at your wife. I don't have to lift a finger. You shall reap what you sow," Jacob said opening the door.

Wayne walked through and Jacob slammed the door behind him. He banged his fist against the door and screamed. Then he picked up Wayne's whiskey glass and threw it against the door, smashing it to pieces. He tried to calm down, went over to the sofa and poured himself another glass. His hands were shaking. Molly would be home soon from the sitter. He rubbed his hands on his face and then wiped the sweat off on his trousers.

By the time Molly arrived home, he was a bit tipsy, but much calmer. He had decided that he would visit the sisters in the morning. Maybe they could plead the case for him and it wouldn't seem so much his idea. There was some air of distrust toward Catholics in the area, but these were nuns, women who had devoted their lives to the service of the Lord. And they were such kind, old women. They were his only hope for saving the orphanage project.

The next morning, Jacob stopped by the office to let Matthew know he would be in later that afternoon. He rode over to an area of town called The Northern Liberties. It was populated by bootleggers, drunkards, prostitutes and petty thieves. There in the basement of an old warehouse, the sisters had set up shop. He stepped down from the wagon and nearly fell into a pile of pig dung. The smell of rotting meat filled the air. This was no place to raise a child, thought Jacob. He walked down the old concrete steps and knocked at the door. He heard a woman's voice ask

"Who's there?"

"It's Jacob Hoffner, ma'am. I've come to speak with Sister Catherine," he replied.

He heard a lock turn, and he was ushered inside. A large cold room stood before him lined with old picnic tables, seated were dozens of tiny children, dirty and wearing mismatched clothing. They appeared to be eating some kind of soup. Blankets lined the walls.

That must be where they sleep, thought Jacob. His heart broke at the sight. Most of them were no older than Molly. They stared at him, unaccustomed to having visits from strangers. The woman who opened the door looked no more than 19. She was dressed in a simple habit and had a plain face. There was nothing remarkable about her appearance. He doubted he would recognize her should they meet again. But, she offered to go fetch Sister Catherine. Two nuns minded the children, who were eating. The sisters seemed stern, but kind. He saw one pat a small boy on the head and place his empty soup bowl on the table reserved for dirty dishes.

A few minutes later, Sister Catherine emerged from a side room. She was elderly, but vibrant. She had an energy about her that superseded her age. She had small eyes and a German accent. When she spoke, Jacob stood at attention as if he was a child again listening to his mother.

"Ah, Mr. Hoffner," she said. "I hope you come with good news," she said hopefully.

"I'm afraid not, Sister Catherine," Jacob replied. "It seems I've met some opposition from the Presbyterians. They favor new church pews over the building of a Catholic orphanage. I've come to ask for your assistance. These children here are in such need. I thought perhaps if you came and pleaded your case, perhaps brought a little one or two with you, they would change their hearts. What do you think?" Jacob asked.

"I think we could do that. I'm sorry to hear you've been shunned. People can be so touchy about religious differences. But, we're all here to serve God, are we not?" she said.

"Yes, ma'am. I hope to come through for you. Can you come to the lodge tomorrow evening around 6:00 p.m.?" Jacob asked.

"Yes, that will be fine. Thank you for coming by."

She showed him to the door, and Jacob took one last look back at the sad little faces. He walked out onto the street and a woman with thick rouge and a ruffled black skirt tapped him on the shoulder.

"Like to come up to my room for a good time, old man? I'm real good," she whispered in his ear.

She looked no more than 16. Jacob said not a word and handed her a dollar. Then he got into the wagon, shook the reigns and rode away as quickly as he could. How could these children be expected to grow up to be respectable citizens living in an area like that? They had no future. The girls would grow up to be prostitutes and the boys thieves. Something had to be done. He hoped the sisters could turn this around.

The next day Sister Catherine arrived at the Masonic Hall in a carriage with a 5 year old boy and a 7 year old girl in tow. A crowd of members of the Order met the carriage and Jacob assisted Sister Catherine off of the wagon into the hall. As the Grandmaster called the meeting to order, Sister Catherine sat quietly in the corner on a bench with her two young charges. The Grandmaster, Nicholas Brundy, called the meeting to order and explained that today they would take a vote on the use of funds after hearing the two proposals.

Jacob began, "I have brought with me today Sister Catherine from the sisters of St. Francis. They have been running an orphanage in The Northern Liberties in the most desperate of conditions. I ask that you hear what the sister has to say before making a decision."

The Grandmaster nodded. Sister Catherine stepped forward with the two children.

"With the outbreaks of tuberculosis and cholera in our community, men who have died in factory accidents and pregnant wives who die in childbirth, our community has close to 100 children without family to care for them. My sisters and I have done what we can with our meager funds to make these children comfortable. But, they often go without food, sleep on blankets on the hard floor. We do not have ample heating in the building and are subject to overcrowding. The children spread illness quickly because they are in such close quarters and many of them don't make it.

Young Caroline here was a member of the Jefferson family and her father was a fine factory worker. But, his wife was nine months pregnant when he fell into a large compactor at work and in grief, she labored early and passed. Young Charlie here was the son of a merchant whose wife died years ago, but the merchant was run over in the street while crossing late at night. These children come from good families and deserve homes. I ask for mercy on their souls," she concluded.

Many of the members seemed moved by her speech and examined the children with looks of pity.

Wayne spoke next, "These children are nothing but paid street performers, the children of liars and thieves. This woman – everyone knows that Catholics worship idols – saints, Mary – is idolatrous. She cannot be trusted. She's an instrument of the devil sent to tempt us by this known heathen Jacob Hoffner. Do not believe a word of it. All of you Christian men will make the righteous choice – the installation of new pews to comfort our elderly Christian relatives. It is the only honorable proposal," he ended.

Several of Wayne's friends seemed confounded by the speech, unsure of whom to believe. But, Sister Catherine had an aura of purity about her and they weren't quick to believe Wayne's claims. The Grandmaster called for the vote. 25 in favor of the orphanage, 21 in favor of the church pews. Wayne stormed out in disgust. Jacob felt relieved, smiled and escorted Sister Catherine to her wagon. He promised to update her just as soon as the construction plans were underway.

Jacob rested easily that night. It seemed all his problems had melted away. Sometimes right does win out in the end, he thought. He didn't feel the eyes peering at him through his window, vowing revenge upon him and cursing his name.

13

As Anna drove up to the cemetery that morning, she felt angry. She felt the ghost had been playing a game with her, and she was tired of playing. Her life seemed to be in shambles, she wasn't speaking to Patrick, she was about to get fired for missing work. *And for what? A lousy diary.* She must be losing her mind. She stomped across the gravel, plopped down on the steps and yelled,

"What? What do you want, old man? I did what you asked I got the diary. Now what?"

She was frustrated and frowning. She ranted about what a mess her life had become. Jacob appeared, tranquil as ever at the foot of the statue and simply gazed at her and her tantrum. She threw a handful of pebbles at him, but they went through him and landed on the ground.

"Can I say something?" asked the ghost.

She stopped gesturing, calmed down and said, "sure."

"It seems like you were already having some problems, before I asked you to do anything. I was only trying to help," he said.

She began to interject and then stopped herself.

"You know I know what it feels like to be

misunderstood. When I was alive, I did a great deal of good for this community. That has all long been forgotten. There were rumors about me that some people continued to believe to my grave. I want to set the record straight. You want to be a writer. I thought we could strike a deal. I have my story told, fulfilling my legacy. You write the book, fulfilling yours. What do you think?"

He sat and waited for her response. She stammered,

"Write a book? But, I'm not a writer; you want a real writer, someone professional. I can't do this. I haven't written anything longer than a short story. I'm sorry, you have the wrong girl," she said resolutely.

"Oh, but I don't," said Jacob. "You forget that I can see all. I know what you've done, what you've felt, what you've seen, what you've said. You're right. Your life is a mess. But, I've seen how you write and I know you are capable of great emotion. That's what I want, someone that can picture my story, feel what I felt and relay it on paper. I don't want a copy of my diary; I want a retelling of it, with drama and suspense and heart. Buried underneath all this insecurity and muck you show to the world, you have a good heart. And that is why I have chosen you," said Jacob.

Anna was stunned. She didn't know what to say. She felt flattered or honored or both.

She sat for a few moments in somber reflection. Hadn't this been what she always wanted? This was her chance to make something of herself. She just needed to pull herself together, apologize to Patrick, write this book and go forward. She felt better than she had felt in days. At long last, she said "I would be honored."

"Good," Jacob said. "I look forward to hearing the first draft. Come back when you have it completed."

She nodded and went on her way still feeling reticent but more confident about herself. She pulled into the parking lot, resolved to patch things up with Patrick. She had been acting crazy the last few days, and he had been nothing but kind to her. She bounded up the stairs and unlocked the door.

Something seemed off when she walked in. It was just a feeling, but then she noticed the panties on the floor. They weren't hers. She could hear laughter coming from the bedroom. She threw open the door and found Patrick in their bed with Ashley riding him like a carnival ride. He stopped in mid thrust and stared at her. Her eyes were wild. She said nothing. She ran from the room, down the stairs, out to the car. She drove through a red light, tires screeching and pulled over.

She burst into tears. The bastard, she was so stupid. She realized she had done the same thing to him, but that was with someone who meant nothing to her. She had seen the way he looked at Ashley, his hand on the small of her back, the way she had flirted with him. This was something more than a one night mistake. Snot began to run down her face with her tears. She couldn't breathe. She didn't want to go back to the apartment. She never wanted to see him again. She wasn't sure where she should go, so she decided to call Midge.

"Oh honey, you poor thing," Midge said. "You come right over, now, you hear? I'll make you some chili, fix you right up. Stay as long as you like."

Anna said she would be over shortly. First she stopped by a donut shop, cramming chocolate glazed donut after chocolate glazed donut into her mouth. The food numbed the pain a little. A few minutes later, she was ringing the doorbell of Midge's little ranch house with an old lawn jockey in the front.

"Come in sugar. I got the guest room all ready for ya. I'll drive you to work in the morning. Everything's going to be all right."

She gave Anna a big hug and told her to go lie down. Midge's poodle, Mitzie, jumped up on the bed and sat on Anna's chest. She petted the little dog and cried herself to sleep. Midge woke her up a couple of hours later, fussing at her to eat some chili and watch some *Wheel of Fortune*. Anna robotically followed her into the dining room and did as she was told. It all seemed like a dream, a bad dream. Anna wished she could rewind time and do things differently. Deep down, she knew she had willed this to happen on some level. She had wanted to be free. But, the reality of it hit her with such blunt force and she felt devastated nonetheless. Midge coddled her the rest of the evening, feeding her cake and pie and calling Patrick a no-good scoundrel.

Anna forgot about her novel, went to work the next day and continued with her regular routine. Patrick left messages on her cell phone, but she didn't listen to them and she didn't call him back. She stayed with Midge and occasionally drove by the apartment to see if Patrick's car was there. One afternoon, she was pleased to see that it wasn't. She went inside; loaded up everything she could into the backseat and trunk of her car and took it to Midge's house. She piled it all up in a corner of the garage. Midge said she could stay with her until she saved up a down payment for a new apartment. Anna thanked Midge over and over for her hospitality. She was a good friend.

After a month had passed, Anna thought about what Jacob had said. She realized she was the architect of her own destruction and felt somehow the writing of this novel might be her only salvation.

Instead of going back to Midge's that evening and watching yet another round of *Jeopardy*, she decided to go to a bookstore. She slunk down in one of the big comfy chairs with a cup of coffee, got out a pen and paper and started to write the beginning of Jacob's story. The words flowed from her fingertips. She could hear his voice in her head and it was more like she was taking dictation than actually writing. It felt good to get her mind off of Patrick and on to something else. When she wrote about the death of Jacob's wife, it felt cathartic. Through her pain, she could feel his pain and express it on the page.

She got in the habit of going to the bookstore regularly, trudging through snow all winter long, writing and writing. Within a month, she had written about the stories in half the diary and then realized she hadn't even read the rest. Reading was so restful. It allowed her mind to wander to all of her problems. Typing kept her mind busy, so she had focused on that instead.

One Tuesday evening, as she was writing, she realized she wasn't feeling well. She ran to the restroom and threw up. She feared she had the flu and stayed home from work the next day. As she laid with her head in Midge's toilet, she realized that she couldn't remember the last time she had her period.

"Oh God," she thought.

She ran out to the drugstore to buy a pregnancy test. She took it, it was positive. She ran back to the drugstore for three more tests. All three had the same result. She realized the baby either belonged to the stranger at the bar or Patrick and neither seemed a happy prospect.

How was she going to support a child on warehouse wages? She thought about aborting it, but after reading pages upon pages about Jacob's love for Molly, she just couldn't do it. She wanted the baby, however it came to be.

When Midge came home that evening, she talked it over with her. Midge was a little shocked, coming from a different generation where a woman raising a baby alone simply wasn't done. But, she vowed her support. Anna nearly had enough money for a down payment on a new apartment, but no money for medical expenses. She didn't know what she was going to do. She felt bad for putting Midge out and didn't want to stay there much longer. She became irritable and depressed, spent long periods of time in bed and got cross with Midge and her mothering.

Brad was on her last nerve at work. She didn't tell him the news, fearing he would make her take an early leave when her pregnancy forced her to slow down her production rate. Brad wasn't going to make any accommodations for a pregnant woman around heavy machinery. She was tired and defeated.

She didn't know what else to do. So, she went back to the bookstore, the one place where she was able to forget about her troubles. She curled up in a ball and began reading the rest of Jacob's diary. She hoped the story had a happy ending.

14

It was the night of Molly's play, *A Midsummer Night's Dream*. Entering the auditorium, it looked like a magical forest with candle sconces hung from the ceiling and a cardboard set cut out to look like trees and painted by the children on stage. Jacob took a program and made his way to his seat. The curtain opened. The fairy dresses sparkled, the children remembered their lines -- give or take a line or two. Jacob laughed. He hadn't laughed in a long time.

He briefly thought of Sarah and how proud she would be of her daughter. He thought of Elizabeth and how proud she would be of her niece. He felt lucky that he was still here and able to laugh with Molly and see her shine.

He was mid-chuckle as he watched the kid dressed as the donkey trip on stage when he caught sight of Wayne out of the corner of his eye. Wayne's face furrowed with anger. Jacob then realized the kid playing the donkey was Wayne's son and his chuckle dissolved into seriousness. Wayne turned back around to watch the performance. Helen, sitting next to him, turned around to see what he had been looking at. When she saw Jacob, she averted her eyes nervously and turned back around.

When the show was over, Jacob hustled backstage with a bouquet of flowers for Molly. She ran out from behind the curtain and he gave her a big hug.

"You were great!" he exclaimed.

Molly said, "Really, you really think so? You're not just saying that, Papa?"

She looked dubious.

"Nope, God's honest truth – you stole the show," he replied.

They walked hand in hand back to the wagon, Molly waving excitedly at her classmates as they walked out the doors. As Jacob helped Molly into the carriage, he spotted Wayne walking toward him with purpose. Helen grabbed him by the arm and pulled him aside. Jacob set off with an uneasy feeling in the pit of his stomach.

He got home and got Molly to bed. He wasn't tired, so he went and poured himself a glass of whiskey and sat in the kitchen reading by lamplight. Around midnight, he heard a soft knock at the door. Not expecting company, he loaded his shotgun and walked cautiously toward it.

"Who's there?" he called out.

"It's Helen," a frightened female voice replied.

"Helen? Are you alone?" Jacob asked.

"Yes, yes. Please let me in. Something dreadful has happened."

He threw open the door to find Helen standing in the darkness, blood covering her cotton dress. She was sobbing, tears and snot were running down her face and she appeared to be having trouble breathing. He took her arm and led her to a chair. She put her face in her hands and rocked back and forth.

"Helen? What is it Helen? Is it one of your children? Has something happened? Should I call for help? What is it Helen?" Jacob asked anxiously trying to get some sort of response.

"It's Wayne. He's dead," Helen blubbered.

He went and soaked a rag with cold water to rub against her hot cheeks.

"Dead? What happened?" Jacob asked.

He gave her a few minutes to catch her breath. When she had calmed herself down and wiped her eyes, she told him what happened.

Wayne had been angry when they returned home, cross with the children and spitting venom at Helen about how Jacob had laughed at his son, how Jacob was ruining his chances at becoming Grandmaster, how Helen really wanted to be with Jacob instead of him. He struck her across the face. She told the children to run to the neighbor's house and stay there. They were frightened and crying, not wanting to leave their mother, but she pleaded for them to go.

"I've seen how you look at him, that heathen! I bet you like the old man with his grey eyes and his pockets loaded with money!" Wayne had screamed at her.

"No, I swear. He is only kind to me. But you – you are not. I will not stay here any longer. I don't care what they say about me. You're a hateful man. I will not raise my children with a hateful man!" she screamed.

He shoved her to the ground with his arms around her throat. He began choking her.

"Oh yeah, they're your children now, are they? What are you going to do leave me and raise them with him? Oh, you'll not do that, you strumpet. I'll see you in Hell first. And then I'll send Jacob there after you. And you can writhe in your sin together for eternity," Wayne sneered.

Helen couldn't breathe. She thought of her children. She was angry, so angry for all the years of abuse she had endured. She wasn't going to let Wayne kill her and Jacob, the only man who had ever been kind to her. She wasn't going to let that monster raise her children. She scooted along the floor, nearly about to lose consciousness. She grabbed the concrete statue of an angel that sat underneath the end table. Wayne screamed and choked her. She raised the statue above her head and cracked him as hard as she could in the skull.

Wayne's hands released from her neck, and he fell backward. She could hear him still breathing. She picked up the statue and hit him with it over and over again. After the fifth blow, his eyes glazed over. She stopped and stared at him. She stared at the blood on her dress and realized what she had done.

As Helen ended her story, she looked up at Jacob.

"I ran straight here," she told Jacob as she wiped the tears from her eyes. I didn't know what else to do."

She explained that she was afraid the police would think she had murdered him and she would hang for it.

"I'm so scared," she whimpered.

Jacob was in shock. He grabbed them both a glass of bourbon.

"Can I examine you for a minute?" he said.

She looked at him quizzically, but nodded. He put his fingers gently on her neck. She flinched.

"I'm not going to hurt you, I promise," he said turning her neck from side to side.

There were fingernail marks on her skin and deep bruises beginning to form around her neck.

"You need to go home and call the police," he said.

"Why . . . but I can't. I can't go back there," she said.

"It will look bad if you stay here," he replied. "It will look like you're guilty of something more. But, the marks on your neck are prominent. They'll believe it was self-defense. But you must go now – before the body starts to set. You were never here," he said.

Helen said, "I understand. Thank you for your help," and walked toward the door.

"Of course, I will do anything to help you," Jacob said. "Let me know if you need anything."

With that, she walked out the door. He shut it behind her and sat in stunned silence for the remainder of the night.

15

Anna was in the midst of reading the murder scene, when a young brunette woman with glasses walked up and tapped on her shoulder. She jumped into the air.

"You startled me," she said to the bookstore clerk.

"We're closing in 15 minutes," the clerk replied.

"O.K. Thanks," Anna replied.

This journal is getting exciting, Anna thought. For a couple of hours she had forgotten about all of her own troubles.

She patted her stomach lovingly. *I better make an appointment with the doctor,* she thought. She was three months along and would probably start showing soon. What was she going to do with this baby? What kind of mother would she be? She really needed to get her act together for the sake of the child. She thought about her job at the warehouse. That just wasn't going to be feasible much longer. She needed to find a new job. She was glad tomorrow was Sunday. The weekend was not yet over and she had some hours still to think about a plan.

The bookstore clerk eyed her with an annoyed expression on her face. Anna rose slowly and left the bookstore. As she walked along the sidewalk to her car, she felt a man brush against her shoulder.

"Anna," Patrick said. "We need to talk," he said.

"I don't have anything to say to you," Anna replied and turned her shoulder.

"Anna, please. I just want to explain," he said.

She couldn't look at him.

"Save it," she said. "You and I both know it just wasn't meant to be."

She pulled her coat around herself and walked briskly to the car. She had to get out of this town. She couldn't let Patrick know she was pregnant. She would never be free.

She drove to a nearby coffee shop, walked in and found a table near the back. The dark haired hipster waitress meandered her way over to the table and took her order for a white chocolate mocha. She slid out of her coat, straightened her sweater and looked around. Couples were drinking coffee and staring into each other's eyes. A young student was typing away on a keyboard. Three girls, covered in tattoos and animated with youthful rebellion were talking about a concert at the table behind her.

Anna felt lonely and out of sorts. She wanted to go back and see Jacob, but didn't think she should until she finished the first draft. She pulled out her laptop and continued typing where she left off.

Her thoughts turned to Patrick. She knew the right thing to do would be to tell him about the baby. But, she wasn't even sure it was his or if it was the guy from the club. She knew he would do the right thing and give her child support, come for regular visits. But, she had a feeling he wasn't the father. There was no need to ruin his life and hers with a possibility. They would just make each other miserable.

Anna stared at her white chocolate mocha and wondered how much caffeine it contained. She dug in her purse for her cell phone and left a message with her OB GYN to see if she could get an appointment for the next morning. The on call nurse called her back and said they had an opening around 9:00. Anna turned her attention back to her draft and cranked out a few pages. Then her daydreams got the better of her and she started looking for places to live. She had always dreamed of living by the ocean, smelling the salty air, waking up to the sound of seagulls and the waves crashing against the beach. Anna hadn't been on a vacation in a very long time. She started researching beaches along the East Coast and liked the look of the Outer Banks in North Carolina. It seemed remote, peaceful, off the beaten path and not in the midst of hundreds of tourists.

Maybe that's what she needed – a change of scenery to clear her head and figure out her next steps. She remembered how excited she had been when she took the short jaunt to Indiana. A week on the beach might just the thing she needed. Her vacation time had reset at the beginning of the year, so she had her full two weeks. She was going to quit anyway. There was nothing to lose by asking Brad. She started searching for rental properties and found a small one bedroom cottage with a porch overlooking the ocean.

But, she was broke. How was she going to pay for it? Maybe Midge would loan her some money if she asked. She could promise that she would come back with a plan and be out of her hair within the month. Anna emailed the cottage owners to check on availability the next week. She realized she was procrastinating from the task at hand. She had to finish this novel. Maybe she could finish it at the cottage! Yes, that was a perfect idea. She gathered up her laptop, paid her tab at the register and hurried home to talk to Midge.

Midge was peeling potatoes when she arrived.

"Hey, sugar, how was your day?" said Midge.

"I made an appointment with the doctor," said Anna.

"Good, you need to get you some of those prenatal vitamins," she said.

"I ran into Patrick at the bookstore," Anna said.

"Did you talk to him?" Midge asked.

"No, there's no point. The baby isn't his anyway. I just have a gut feeling about it," said Anna.

"It might be good to have someone around to help out," said Midge.

"I'll be fine. We'll manage. Hey, Midge, can I ask you a huge favor?" said Anna.

Midge put down her knife to listen. Anna picked it up and started peeling the potatoes for her.

"I think I need to get away for a while, clear my head. So much has happened and I need to figure out a new direction for my life. I found a cottage online at a beach in North Carolina. It's only $100 a night. I think it would do me a world of good. Do you think there is any way you could loan me the money?" she asked with puppy dog eyes.

"I got me a little bit saved up for a rainy day. I suppose I could give it to ya if you promise to pay me back," said Midge.

Anna stopped peeling and gave Midge a big hug.

"Thank you so much. I'll pay you back I swear. I'll straighten myself out and be out of your hair in a month," said Anna.

"I'm not the one you need to worry about, child, good luck telling Brad," Midge said with a worried expression on her face.

"I'll get a note from the doctor. It will be fine, Midge. I just know it," said Anna.

16

Helen did as Jacob had instructed and ran home to get the police. She showed them the marks on her neck. They brought her in for questioning for what felt like hours, but seemed to believe she would get a fair trial. She fetched her children from the neighbor and told them what had happened. They didn't cry for their father. They had been afraid of him most of their lives and seemed relieved to have him gone.

Jacob kept his distance from her, afraid that any attempt at contact at that point would reek of impropriety. He thought of how many times he himself had wished Wayne dead and felt guilty as though somehow he had brought this all about with his thoughts. The Masons were conflicted about how to handle Wayne's funeral. He had been a longstanding member of the Order, but with the trial looming that hinged on his attempt to kill his wife, they weren't eager to show their support. In the end, few people came to the service. The Order sent flowers addressed to the family.

After a few months, Jacob felt it was safe to bring up the matter of the orphanage again. He felt guilty about winning this point because a man had died, but it was too important a cause to abandon. Sister Catherine had checked in on him upon hearing of Wayne's death and reiterated that the children were nearly freezing in the old warehouse. On a Tuesday in May, Jacob approached the Order again with the idea for the orphanage. It seemed Wayne's friends had been swayed by the reports of his ill character leading to his demise and wanted to distance themselves from him. They had a change of heart. And to Jacob's overwhelming joy the vote went in his favor. The construction of the orphanage was to begin within the month.

Jacob himself enjoyed the hard work of construction. He had help constructing his fine home. He had a hired a carpenter from Sweden and a blacksmith from Poland. But, he put the beams in himself and enjoyed doing the crown moldings and other finishing touches. The land chosen for the orphanage belonged to Jacob himself. It was two streets over and two acres with a couple of fine oak trees. Jacob put on his overalls and work boots and accompanied a team of men out to the site to begin work. Molly asked if she could come along, but he asked her to stay with the sitter. He was fearful of having her around during the construction phrase, but promised she could help with the painting.

Sister Catherine came to oversee the work and was nearly in tears she was so excited.

"God Bless you, Mr. Hoffner," she said. "The Lord shall reward thee in Heaven."

He acknowledged her blessing and said he was just doing what he thought best for the little ones. Henry came out to help, as did Matthew.

"It's a delight to see you whistling, Jacob. I don't think I've seen you look this chipper in a good while," said Henry.

"It feels good to have a purpose, Henry. It's good for the soul when you can help out others doing something you love," said Jacob.

Henry agreed.

With that, they set about hammering nails, sawing planks and checking blueprints.

By month's end, the framework of the building was in place. Sister Catherine brought the children out for a visit to see their new home. Their little faces lit up with joy when they saw the rolling hills, trees and fresh air. They inhaled the fragrance of the land as if they smelled cookies bake for the first time. Jacob took them on a tour, explaining where the bedrooms would be, the kitchen and the play area. They couldn't wait to see it and looked near to tears when they had to go back to the squalor of the inner city. Jacob talked to Sister Catherine about the importance of education and how he wanted a good portion of the proceeds to go toward new books and writing tablets. He had always regretted that he never attended college or high school for that matter. He wanted the children to have a good chance at a positive future.

A few weeks later when the windows were being fitted, Jacob spied a familiar face in the reflection as he set the window in its frame. It was Helen! Jacob's heart skipped a little when he saw her, and he nearly dropped the window. She didn't speak until he had it properly set and turned around.

"Hello, Jacob," she said.

"Well, aren't you a lovely sight," he said smiling at her.

And indeed she had a glow about her. She stood up straighter, her expression was more radiant. All those years of being under Wayne's control had contorted her features and dulled her complexion. But now that she was free, Jacob could see that she was truly beautiful.

"I've been reading of the trial in the papers," Jacob said. "I was pleased to hear that you were acquitted."

"As was I, for the children's sake. I still have terrible nightmares about that night. I'm so glad you never came to harm. Thank you so much for helping that dreadful night,

Jacob. I don't know how I can ever repay you," she said.

"Think not of it. That man was trouble. I could see it from the moment I laid eyes on him. I'm just glad you weren't hurt. How are the children?" he asked.

"Oh they're doing fine. They actually seem happier. William is doing better in school and little George is starting to walk. Things are getting easier. We have a little money from the insurance settlement. But, it's not quite enough. I was hoping maybe I could somehow help out with the orphanage," she said.

"Well, what would you like to do?" Jacob asked. "The sisters from what I understand provide most of the care and education of the children."

"I'm a good cook," said Helen. "I'm used to making large quantities. My father had a lot of brothers and sisters growing up. Farmhands would often come over for meals. I was the oldest and it was my responsibility to feed them. I make great cornbread and pot of beans," she said.

"Well, I might have to be the judge of that," said Jacob. "I'd like a taste test of this cornbread and pot of beans sometime," said Jacob.

Helen blushed and said, "I would like that very much. How about tonight? Around 7? You can bring Molly if you would like".

"That sounds like a fine idea. I should be good and hungry by the time we finish installing these windows," said Jacob.

"Well, then, I'll go home and start cooking," said Helen.

She smiled, turned and walked away.

Jacob felt the heat rise to his cheeks. He had always told himself his feelings for Helen were entirely platonic and out of care and concern. But his racing heartbeat told another story. It had been a long time since Jacob had courted a woman and he wasn't sure what to do. He hurried home at the end of the day to bathe and find a clean shirt. He carefully combed his graying hair as he stared at his wrinkling reflection in the mirror. He adjusted his tie and his cape.

"Molly are you about ready, sweetheart?" he called out.

Molly walked into the room in her Sunday dress, smiling. She came over and adjusted Jacob's ties.

"You look very fine, Papa," she said and giggled.

"I'm nervous, Molly," he said and wiped his brow with a handkerchief.

"Maybe you should bring her some flowers, Papa – from the garden" said Molly.

He decided that was a good idea and walked into the backyard to cut a bouquet of irises. He watched the sun fade behind the hills with its reflection illuminating the pond. He hoped Elizabeth would be happy for him. He felt a tinge of guilt cutting flowers for another woman, but it had been lonely without female companionship. He sat and stared at the sky for a few minutes as if he was watching the Almighty himself.

Molly came up behind him and tapped him on the shoulder.

"Are you ready?" she asked.

"Yes, Molly. Yes, I think I am."

17

The next morning, Anna called Brad rather than going in. She cowardly left a message on his voicemail explaining that she had a medical emergency and would be away for a week. She promised to return with a doctor's excuse. Satisfied that she didn't have to worry about that anymore, she drove herself to her doctor's appointment. She was somewhat nervous and concerned. She hadn't taken excellent care of herself the last three months. She'd had some drinks, her diet could use improvement and her sleeping was erratic. She hoped that the baby was alright.

She sat in the waiting room tapping her foot and watching a rerun of an old *Dr. Phil* show. She filled out the chart which had way too many personal questions for her taste and sat back down.

Finally after thirty minutes of waiting, a nurse came to the door and called, "Anna Perrault, the doctor will see you now."

Anna walked back to the small room, undressed and sat on the paper covered examination chair in her paper robe. It felt like an eternity before she heard a knock at the door asking if it was O.K. to come in.

Dr. Wheeler was a tall, business-like blonde woman with glasses and she strode over to her side with purpose. She looked at Anna's chart, commented on it and asked several questions about her last period and how she was feeling. Anna had lied a little on the chart. She really didn't think her sex life was any of the doctor's business.

"Well, let's see what we have going on here," she said as she rolled her chair toward Anna's legs to examine her. "We'll do blood tests to confirm everything is O.K. but I feel a baby down here. You're three months along. We should be able to hear the heartbeat by now. Would you like to hear it?" she asked.

Anna nodded, and the doctor pressed the stethoscope against her stomach. She could hear the rapid "whoosh, whoosh" sound of the baby's heartbeat. Her own heart melted. It suddenly all seemed so real. Tears fell down her cheeks.

"Sounds like it might be a girl. If I was a betting woman, that's what I would bet. We will know around 20 weeks. Here are some prenatal vitamins and an order for your labs to take to the hospital," she said.

Anna sat up, stunned and not saying much.

"Congratulations," Dr. Wheeler said as she walked out the door so Anna could dress.

Anna felt like she might leap out of her skin. She dressed herself, paid her copay and went to the hospital to get her labs. She hated giving blood and winced when the needle pierced her skin. By the time she got back in her car she was exhausted from the ordeal and couldn't wait to get away. She went home and ate some lunch and then started packing. *This might be the last time I wear a bikini for a while*, she thought as she tossed it in the suitcase. She added shorts, t-shirts, sandals, journals, and pens.

Oh, I almost forgot, she thought, tossing the prenatal vitamins in before zipping up the suitcase.

When she got on the road it was mid-afternoon, traffic was heavy. She turned on the radio to occupy her mind until the signal cut out. The drive through Kentucky was scenic and peaceful. When she crossed the Tennessee border, she noticed that the terrain became more mountainous and she needed to pay closer attention as she drove around the curves. She could no longer find a radio station she liked and switched to her iPod.

It started to get dark as she approached Asheville. Mountains loomed in the distance. They seemed majestic and powerful, the exact opposite of how she felt at the moment. She began to sing along to the music and rolled down the window to keep awake. She thought about driving straight through, but she was getting tired and thought that unwise considering the baby. She started searching the exit signs for a hotel and found a Hampton Inn located at the next exit. She parked the car, got out and stretched. She could feel the strain in her neck from driving for hours. She entered the lobby through the automatic doors and approached the wooden counter to inquire about a room.

The groggy clerk asked her if she had a reservation and then said they had 1 smoking room available near the pool. *Smoking room?* She was surprised those still existed, but she was tired and said she would take it. She walked down the hall and to the right, slid her key card in the door and dragged her suitcase into the room. She flopped down on the queen size bed and turned on the TV. She watched a couple of reruns of *Friends* and then realized she couldn't sleep.

She wandered down the hall to the lobby and found a snack machine. She got a bag of peanut m & m's and a Coke and went to sit on a bench. She noticed an old man with an Indian accent checking in. He walked past her dragging his carry-on behind him and then stopped for a minute. She looked up as she popped a yellow m & m into her mouth.

"You really should be drinking water in your condition," he said.

She was a little thrown that he knew she was pregnant. He sat down next to her. Normally, she would be disturbed if a stranger sat down next to her. But, this man seemed to emanate a feeling of peace and she was not afraid of him.

He looked her in the eyes and said, "She will be beautiful and magnificent. Take care of her, for she is your legacy."

Then he stood up and continued dragging his carry-on to his room. She felt strange as if some angelic presence had just visited or as if she had received a message from the divine. She stood up and threw the rest of the m & m's away. She walked to her room, changed into her pajamas and tried to sleep. This adventure was already getting interesting.

The next morning, she dressed quickly in order to enjoy the free breakfast buffet before it ended at 10:00. She loaded her plate with eggs and fruit and for the first time in a long while, had water to drink. The words of the strange Indian man kept ringing in her head. They made her feel better somehow, as if everything was going to be O.K. She checked out, put her suitcase in the car and continued her drive across North Carolina. The mountains were beautiful in the morning sunshine. The grass was a vibrant green and the sky a glorious blue. She zipped along, singing "Walking on Sunshine" by Katrina and the Waves. At times, she would talk to the baby.

"You should see these mountains little one, so beautiful, so magnificent – like you."

After a couple of hours, the terrain evened out as she made her way into the heart of North Carolina. She stopped in Chapel Hill for lunch and took a few minutes to walk around the quaint college town. She enjoyed watching the college students shop and duck into coffee houses. They seemed like they were brimming with life, possibilities and dreams. The further she traveled the more her problems seemed to disappear with each road sign. She felt like she could think more clearly and she felt more hopeful.

By midafternoon, she arrived at the Outer Banks. She wanted to go straight to the cottage but could not contain her excitement upon seeing the ocean. She parked at the public beach landing and hopped out of the car and ran straight down the boardwalk. The sun was high in the sky. There were a few children playing in the sand making sandcastles. The wind blew forcefully off the surf. She closed her eyes and listened to the roar of the waves. She sat down on the edge of the boardwalk and stared out as far as the eye could see. It was so beautiful. She hadn't been to the beach in such a long time and had forgotten how beautiful it was. She sat for nearly an hour staring in awe at the sight of it. Then, remembering why she had come, she walked back to the car to look at her directions.

It appeared that the cottage was only two miles away. She typed the address into her GPS and put the car in drive. She loved the color of houses near the beach. They were always so light and pastel – airy like meringue. She drove down the street watching pedestrians in beach wraps walking on the sidewalks making their way down to the ocean. She was so happy to be away from home. "You have arrived," said her GPS in its electronic female voice.

She eyed the cottage, quite rustic, blue with chipping paint. She walked up to the cracked cement porch and opened the squeaky screen door. No air conditioning – well, what did she expect for the price? She walked in and found a small kitchen to the right with a tiny gas oven and small sink, one cabinet. To the left was a small bedroom, with a twin size bed, and small closet. The living room contained a wicker chair, a gaudy couch with a wild Hawaiian plant design and a television. She eyed the sliding glass doors behind the vertical blinds. She set her suitcase down and walked over to examine them. She tugged on the handle and pulled the door to the left. She could feel the ocean breeze as she stepped out into the sunlight. She slipped off her shoes and dug her toes into the sand. *Right on the beach - perfect*. She forgot any flaws she had found with her new abode. It was exactly where she wanted to be. She walked out onto the deserted stretch of beach behind the dwelling. She walked down to the ocean's edge, stuck her toes in the surf and let the cool water rush over them. She smiled and skipped back to the cottage.

She set up shop quickly and made herself at home. She threw her clothes into the dressers and set her toiletries out on the bathroom sink. She peeled herself out of her jeans that were becoming much too tight on her belly and threw on a pair of shorts. She pulled Jacob's diary out of her suitcase, grabbed a beach towel and walked out back onto the beach. Anna carefully laid her towel down putting her sandals on the ends to keep it from blowing away. She laid down for a minute and just absorbed the warm rays of the sun into her face. It felt heavenly. She almost wanted to nap instead of read. She gently flipped the yellowed pages to the place where she had left off. Jacob was building the orphanage and about to have dinner at Helen's house for the very first time.

18

Helen opened the door wearing a white dress with a small red flower pattern. Her hair was curled and pinned up in the back. She smiled when she saw Jacob and greeted Molly with a hug.

"Come in. I'm so happy you two could come," she said.

"Molly, William, Michael and John are playing cowboys and Indians in the backroom if you would like to join them".

Molly looked hesitant to leave Jacob's side, but he gave her a pat on the back and she followed where Helen's finger had pointed.

Helen noticed that Jacob was holding flowers, "Oh how lovely. Let me find a vase. Come in and make yourself comfortable."

She walked away to a side room and left Jacob in the parlor. His eye gazed around the room at the nice but simple furnishings. The coffee table had ornately carved legs but showed signs of wear. A couple of watercolors adorned the walls. He could smell the scent of cornbread waft in from the other room. He sat down in a rocking chair and began to nervously rock back and forth.

A few minutes later, Helen emerged from the kitchen with a vase of irises and set them on the coffee table.

"Would you like some tea, Jacob?" she asked.

Jacob shuffled nervously in his seat, "That would be nice," he replied.

"Earl Grey or Darjeeling?" Helen asked.

"Earl Grey sounds great," said Jacob.

Helen disappeared again.

Jacob hummed to himself and listened to the children in the back room saying "Bang Bang, I got you now, bad guys!"

Helen returned with two cups of tea and sat in an armchair next to Jacob.

"Lovely weather we've been having," he said politely.

She nodded, seeming as nervous as he felt.

"Listen, Jacob. I know this must be awkward for you. It's a very strange situation, I know. I'm not expecting anything. I simply wanted to repay you for your kindness with a hot meal," Helen said.

"Oh, likewise. It's not awkward, Helen. It was very kind of you to invite me over. It's just that I haven't been in the company of a lady in some time," said Jacob.

"You, Jacob?" said Helen. "I'm surprised. I always thought you to be such a handsome man."

Jacob blushed.

"I better check on the beans," said Helen. "I don't want to burn them. Then, you'll never hire me down at the orphanage."

Jacob wondered whether he should follow her. He felt strange being left alone in the room that had once been Wayne's house. Just then, Molly bounded in riding a stick with a horse's head on the top. Three boys wearing feathers on their heads ran behind her whooping and hollering.

"Uncle Jacob, save me!" Molly squealed.

He grabbed her up in his arms and stared down at the boys.

"I'll save you little lassie. Bang. Bang." he said.

He pretended to shoot at the boys. They dramatically clutched their chests and fell to the floor.

Helen yelled "Dinner" from the kitchen and the children ran out of the living room into the dining room, yelling "Coming." Jacob slowly got up and followed them. Candles were lit on the tabletop. A fresh tablecloth had been laid out for the occasion. Jacob waited for the others to take their seats before sitting down. He sat across from Helen and could see the blue of her eyes glint in the candlelight. They held hands and Helen said grace. The children devoured the cornbread and beans, shoveling it into their mouths with their tiny hands. Helen helped the baby, George, and lovingly spooned the food into his chubby cheeks. Jacob ate slowly, appreciating the sight, enjoying the feeling of having a lot of people gathered around the table to break bread.

The cornbread really was delicious, just the right mixture of buttery and sweet, light and fluffy with a bit of grainy cornmeal taste. The beans were cooked with bacon and were soft but not overcooked.

"Why, I do believe this is the best meal I've had in a year," Jacob said.

Helen beamed, "Oh, you're just saying that."

Jacob said, "Oh no, I really mean it. It's delicious. I do believe you're hired Mrs. Gehringer," he said.

"Duvall," Helen replied. "Helen Duvall – I had it changed back to my maiden name."

"Well, then you're hired, Ms. Duvall," said Jacob.

After dinner, Jacob helped Helen clear the dishes. Their hands brushed slightly as they reached for the same plate. Jacob felt a tingle run through his skin. The children went back to William's room to tell ghost stories in the dark with a solitary candlestick. He could hear their giggles and whispering voices. He hoped Molly wouldn't be too scared.

"You're really good with her," Helen said as she

washed the dishes in the sink and Jacob helped dry.

"Who? Molly?" Jacob said.

"Yes, you're a natural with her. Who'd have a thought a man could be so good with a little girl?" said Helen.

"Oh well, she's easy. She doesn't cause me any trouble, always has a smile on her face," said Jacob.

"I always wanted a girl," said Helen. "We kept trying, but I got four boys out of the deal," said Helen.

"They seemed like they turned out pretty good. Good looking boys – they look like their mother," said Jacob.

Helen smiled. "Would you like to sit in the parlor and have some dessert before you go? I made apple pie" she asked.

"Well, I never could turn down a piece of apple pie," Jacob said.

They retreated to the parlor and sat down to enjoy their pie.

"How's the construction coming along? When do you expect the orphanage to be completed?" asked Helen.

"We should have it ready in about three weeks for the children to move in. Of course, we'll still need to work on the inside some more, do some painting and install shelves, that sort of thing. I can introduce you to Sister Catherine tomorrow, if you would like. You two can work out some sort of arrangement for when you can start. I'll give you a glowing recommendation," said Jacob.

"I appreciate that," said Helen. It was silent for a few minutes as neither one of them knew what to say.

"Helen, would you maybe like to go out sometime without the children? I have a nice sitter, a German woman who lives nearby who watches Molly while I'm at meetings. I'm sure she wouldn't mind watching the boys one evening if you would like to go see a show in town," said Jacob.

"Why I haven't seen a show in years!" exclaimed Helen. "Oh what fun! Why I'd love to," said Helen.

"It's a date then," said Jacob.

"It's a date," said Helen.

He pulled out his pocket watch and looked at the time.

"Well, it's getting late. I better get Molly home to bed and I'm sure you're little one is about to get fussy in his crib," said Jacob.

"O.K. well, I'll come by tomorrow to meet Sister Catherine," said Helen.

"I look forward to it. Molly! Time to go!" he yelled into the back room.

Molly bounced into the front room, "Aww . . . do we have to? I was just getting ready to tell the story about the claw!" she exclaimed.

"The claw?" said Jacob shaping his arm into a claw and chasing her out the front door. He turned around and waved at Helen,

"I'll see you tomorrow. Thank you for dinner. It was lovely," he said.

"See you tomorrow," said Helen as she closed the door.

The next day after Jacob sent Molly off to school, he went to check on his business for a few hours. Matthew had stopped working on the construction project to take over the work that needed to be done at the office. Matthew was in the back room stocking shelves when Jacob walked in. He caught Jacob up to date on the ledgers.

"Can I ask you a question, Matthew?" asked Jacob.

"Certainly," said Matthew.

"Do you think it would be O.K. if I started courting Helen?" he asked.

Matthew stared at him dumbfounded. "Well, I don't object to it. I'm just surprised is all. Good for you, I wish you the best of luck," said Matthew.

"But, do you think the Order would look down upon it?" asked Jacob.

"Even if they did, I doubt anyone would say anything

about it. Wayne's no longer around. A dead man cannot lay a claim on her. If you take a fancy to her, you should go for it. You're not getting any younger," said Matthew.

"It's just . . . I've not been with anyone since Elizabeth. What if when the time comes I've forgotten how to do it?" he asked.

"Like riding a horse, my man. Like riding a horse," Matthew laughed and slapped him on the back. Jacob helped Matthew finish stocking and then asked him if he needed any more help.

"I've got it covered. Go on down to the construction site. Let's get that place finished, so I can have you back here full time," Matthew joked.

A couple of hours later, Jacob was installing the front door when he saw Sister Catherine's carriage pull up. He finished screwing in the hinges and then went over to greet her.

"Why Jacob! You've done such a fine job. I love it and it's such a lovely red, so welcoming and inviting," she said admiring the door.

"I think we might finish within the next two weeks," said Jacob.

He looked up with concern at the sky. The clouds were darkening on the horizon.

"It looks like it might start to rain, Sister. Would you like to come back to my house for a cup of tea so we can talk?" Jacob asked.

"I believe you're right. Yes, I do. Is it far?" she said.

"No, ma'am – just a couple of blocks. Jacob and Sister Catherine walked rapidly to his house and dashed in the front door as thunder started to boom in the sky. Rain exploded from the sky and furiously beat against the window panes.

"It looks like we got inside just in time," said Sister Catherine staring out of the window at the dark sky.

Jacob made her a pot of tea on the stove and got out two teacups from the cupboard.

"I can only stay a little while. Then I need to get back to the children. Sister Marietta is in charge at the moment but I'm afraid she can be a little lax with discipline. Hopefully, the storm will pass soon," she said.

"I expect it will. It looks to be one of those flash summer storms that blow in fast and then blow out just as quickly," said Jacob.

"I have a favor to ask of you," said Jacob. "A friend of mine, a woman who has been recently widowed and has four children to take care of, she was wondering if she might be able to have a job as a cook at the orphanage when it opens," said Jacob.

"Well, what a coincidence. It must be God's will. Our cook, Christine has just informed us that she's retiring. So, we're in need of a new cook. Do you know if she's any good?" said Sister Catherine.

"She served me about the best meal I've had in a year the other night," said Jacob. "So, you think it will work out?"

"I don't see why not, you're footing the bill anyway. Hire who you like. She sounds perfect," said Sister Catherine.

"Great. She was supposed to come by the construction site to meet you. I hope she didn't get caught in the rain," Jacob said with a worried look on his face.

"I'm sure she decided to stay in when she saw the storm clouds," assured Sister Catherine.

Then, just as Jacob had predicted the skies parted and a bit of sunlight streamed in through the window.

"You were right, Jacob, a summer flash flood. I'm glad of it. I'll get back to the children and tell them the good news about our new cook," said Sister Catherine.

"Shall I walk you to your carriage?" he asked.

"Oh no, I can manage myself. I think this is the last time I'll stop by before the opening. Please pay us a visit when it's time to move in," she said and let herself out the door.

About fifteen minutes later, a knock came at the door. Jacob went to answer it and found Helen on his doorstep.

"Oh no, I've missed her, haven't I?" she fretted.

"I'm afraid you have. But, not to worry – you've got the job!" he exclaimed and invited her in.

"I do?" she said.

"How did you know we were here?" asked Jacob.

"Henry told me he saw you leave with Sister Catherine before the storm started. I'm sorry to have missed her. I really wanted to meet her," said Helen.

"Well, you'll see her a lot when the orphanage opens in two weeks. It will be great to see you so often, Helen," said Jacob.

"I guess you're right. That show you were talking about the other night? When is it?" asked Helen.

"Oh, it starts this Friday. It's called *Dracula*. It's supposed to be a scary tale about a vampire," said Jacob.

"Oh, how frightening! I might have to lean on your arm and cover my eyes," said Helen.

"I think that would be alright," said Jacob. "Why don't you bring the children over at 6:00, I'll tell Greta to fix us all some dinner. Then we'll go out to the show. How does that sound?" said Jacob.

"Splendid," said Helen.

When Helen moved to leave, Jacob became aware of the feeling that he didn't want her to go, that somehow she belonged here with him. He cautioned himself not to rush things and ruin it with her. But, if things kept going the way they were, he just might ask that girl to marry him.

19

Anna was starting to feel sleepy and hot. She was worried she might sunburn. Jacob's diary had swirled up her emotions. It sounded like he was in love, the kind of love you read about in books. She didn't know that kind of love really existed. She had hoped for it with Patrick, but deep down she knew that although she loved him very much at one time, it wasn't the all-encompassing soul love that Jacob seemed to feel for Helen. She decided to roll over onto her stomach for a few moments and then go back inside.

The week lay out before her without routine or requirement. Her mind felt free but also unstructured and at a loss. She went inside to find a notebook and plan some activities. She decided she would stop by the local grocery that afternoon and pick up some provisions and then walk down to the boardwalk that evening to see if there was any entertainment.

The hours passed slowly. Anna sat in the living room and tapped away at the keyboard slowly finishing the first draft of the novel. She yawned and stretched every 500 words or so, feeling restless. Finally, she felt like procrastinating and she was hungry, so she walked the two blocks to the small grocery at the end of the street.

There were only three aisles in the small store aside from the refrigerated units in the back. She grabbed some pretzels, water and some cheese, being more conscious of the baby growing inside her. She wanted chocolate, but was afraid it would melt in the sun. There didn't seem to be anyone else in the store except for the guy at the counter who was seated on a stool bent over a book. She walked up to the counter and he looked up. He was a blonde, young tanned guy, a typical surfer type. She looked down to see what he had been reading.

"Are you reading *Walden*?" she asked incredulously.

"Oh yeah, I'm taking an English class at the community college and we have to read it for class. Have you read it?" he asked.

"Yeah, I read it a long time ago, but it's been on my mind lately," she said, thinking of Jacob.

"I went to the woods because I wished to live deliberately and not when it came time to die, discover I had not lived. I love that line," he said.

"Yeah, me too," Anna said and paid for her purchases. She walked back to the cottage pondering the words of Thoreau.

She realized that up until now she had led a selfish, dysfunctional life filled with negativity of her own doing. She hadn't meant for it to be that way. She just never really believed that things could be any better. She thought that Patrick didn't love her, and she didn't have the love with him that she wanted. But, she stayed because that's what she believed she deserved. She didn't think she could really be a writer, so she took a job at warehouse that she hated. If she could just believe in herself, just endeavor to live the life she imagined – maybe things could turn around and be different. Maybe her daughter (if the Indian man was right about the baby's sex) would grow up believing in herself too.

When she got to the cottage, she put the groceries

inside on the counter and paced about the living room. She walked out onto the beach, threw herself onto the sand and shouted into the air, "What do you want me to do?"

The only sound that came back was the wind and the surf. She tried imagining her ideal life. Vivid images appeared before her mind's eye. She was working in an office, writing, smiling and having coffee. She saw herself coming home to a nice house on the beach, kissing a handsome man who was holding a baby girl. The vision made her smile. She flooded her mind with it, trying to will it into being. Nothing in her real life had changed and yet, she felt lighter. She dozed off and woke up sweating in the hot sun, unsure at first where she was. She noticed the sun was setting and wondered how long she had been out there.

She went inside to shower and change. She smiled at the decorative soaps on the counter. The cottage was small yes, but the owners had taken care to make it seem homey and welcoming. She had packed a sundress that she never wore, as she wasn't really the dress type. But, it seemed to fit her new image of herself, so she put it on and combed her hair. She smiled in the mirror and set off for the boardwalk. She had only walked a few feet when she realized it was chilly in the ocean air without the sunlight, so she went back inside and grabbed a scarf to wrap around her shoulders.

When she arrived at the boardwalk, she discovered a lively scene. There were guitar players with open cases requesting donations while playing soulful tunes. There were stands set up selling cotton candy, hot dogs and ice cream. Couples were walking hand in hand, children were running about playing tag and everyone had a smile. She suddenly didn't feel alone but part of the grand scheme of things. She spotted a hot pretzel vendor and thought that sounded good, so she bought one and took a bite of the hot, salty dough and dipped it into the melted cheese. It was nearly dark when she noticed the full moon over the ocean. She walked further down the boardwalk toward the surf to take a look at it.

The wind caught her skirt and it started to lift in the wind. She frantically patted it down and tried to clamp it to her legs. As she did that, her scarf blew off of her shoulders.

"Oh no!" she cried.

"I got it!" she heard a man's voice yell out from the darkness.

A tall man with dark brown hair of slender build emerged from the darkness with her scarf in his hand.

"Is this yours?" he asked.

Anna attempted to hold onto her skirt and take the scarf at the same time.

"It looks like you're having a little trouble there," he said chuckling.

"Oh, it's just the wind. Would you mind if we walked back toward the food stands where it's a little less windy?" she asked.

"Not a problem. How about I hold the scarf and you hold the skirt?" he asked.

"Sounds like a plan," said Anna.

When they neared the well-lit food court area, Anna noticed that he looked about the same age as her and was wearing a t-shirt that said "Live the Life You've Imagined." Anna pinched herself to make sure she wasn't dreaming. He handed her the scarf.

"Thank you so much for catching it for me. I don't know how you even saw it in the darkness," she said.

"I didn't see it, but I felt it," he replied.

She stared at him for a few minutes almost wanting to reach out and touch him to see if he was just her imagination.

"My name's Ben, What's yours?" he asked.

"My name's Anna," she said.

"It's a pleasure to meet you, Anna," Ben said.

"Are you vacationing in the Outer Banks?" he asked.

"Yes, I'll be here about a week. And you?" she asked.

"I live here actually," he replied.

"So, what are you? One of those beach bums?" she asked.

"No, actually I'm in real estate. I sell beach cottages. Where are you staying?" he asked.

She gave him the address.

"Cute place. I sold it to the owners, a nice retired couple who like to have somewhere to go in the winter. They rent it as a timeshare when they're away," he replied. "Can I walk you home?" he asked.

She agreed and they talked all of the way back. He was so easy to talk to. He talked about how much he loved the ocean. He grew up in Kansas, so as soon as he graduated from high school he came out to North Carolina and got his real estate license. He had been living there ever since. He'd had a few long-term relationships, nothing too serious. He just hadn't met the one yet. He liked to watch *Game of Thrones*, go surfing and play miniature golf.

Anna told him about her love of writing and books. She told him about her failed relationship with Patrick. She didn't mention the baby, afraid she would scare him off. He listened intently and showed enthusiasm for her taste in music and movies.

By the time they arrived at her cottage door, Anna had the sense that she had known Ben all of her life.

"Think you might be interested in some beachfront property?" Ben asked.

"Oh, I don't think I could afford that," she replied.

"Maybe I could show you a few places anyway. Do you have plans tomorrow?" he asked.

"No, not really – just relaxing. I think I can spare some time to check out a few places. Don't expect a commission though. I'm merely window shopping," she said.

"Gotcha," Ben replied.

He tied her scarf around her shoulders and wished her a good evening. She watched his shadow fade into the darkness with the screen door half open. When she could see him no longer, she went inside and sat on the couch, perplexed.

Well, this is a surprising turn of events, she thought.

The next morning Ben arrived at 10:00 like he said he would. He was driving a golf cart. She hopped in the side and held on as the cart cruised along the sidewalk down some side streets. He showed her a huge mansion house on a cliff that used to belong to a country music star. He showed her an oceanfront bungalow with elaborate sixties decorations including lava lamps. They laughed and talked like old friends and the hours seemed like minutes.

"And this is the best property by far, you will see today," Ben said.

They entered a beautiful yellow cottage with white trim and a large wraparound porch. The inside was traditional with modern touches. There were stainless steel appliances in the kitchen and a large TV in the bedroom. They walked out on the deck and the view was breathtaking.

"Wow, how much is this place?" Anna asked.

"This place is not for sale," Ben said evasively. "This is my place," said Ben.

Anna tried to stop her mouth from hanging open.

"Really?" she nearly squealed. "Holy crap," she said.

Ben laughed and asked her if she would like a glass of wine. She declined and asked for some water. He asked her if she would like to stay for lunch and eat on the deck. She sat on the deck staring out at the ocean, she stared at Ben walking out the patio doors with her sandwich, and she stared at her glass of water. It was surreal.

"You have a beautiful home," she said. "I wish I could stay here forever," she sighed.

"Why don't you?" Ben asked and leaned in for a kiss.

She tried to resist but she could feel the heat of his breath coming toward her and it was intoxicating. She couldn't stop herself from kissing him. It was like she was always meant to kiss him now and forevermore.

20

Helen arrived with William, Michael, George and John in tow. Greta opened the door for her and welcomed her inside. Greta had prepared a marvelous feast for them all including ham, potatoes and green beans. Molly seemed excited to see the boys and dragged them up to her room to show them her things.

The talk at dinner mainly revolved around the children's day at school. They talked about recess and William and Molly talked about the difficulty of memorizing their multiplication tables.

Jacob and Helen listened to the chatter of the children and merely stared across the table at each other. Every few minutes one of them would look away, coyly flirting with the other.

They both hugged all of the children goodbye and told them to be good for Greta and not give her a bit of trouble. The children practically shoved them out the door, eager to start playing with parents away.

Jacob helped Helen into the carriage and off they went downtown.

"Wayne never took me out," Helen said despondently. "I felt like I was never really living before," she said.

"Well, then, let's start living," Jacob said.

They pulled up to the theater and an usher helped them down from the carriage. Jacob paid for their seats, and they sat in the middle waiting for the curtain to rise. As the lights dimmed, Jacob reached for Helen's hand. She wrapped her fingers around his. When the vampire came on stage, Helen gasped and gripped his hand tighter. He never let go. By the end of the performance, her head was resting on his shoulder and they were both smiling. The audience rose to their feet and clapped wildly when the actors came out for bows.

"That was amazing," said Helen.

"I'm glad you liked it," said Jacob.

They walked out onto the street holding hands. Jacob could feel the sweat and clamminess but didn't want to let go. When they arrived home, he walked her to the door and stopped a few feet from the entryway.

"I want to show you something," he said.

He took her hand and walked her around the back. He showed her the gardens, the statues, all the flowers his Elizabeth had loved.

"It's so beautiful. I wouldn't change a thing," said Helen.

He leaned down to kiss her in the moonlight. They touched lips two more times before walking inside to see the children. Jacob was so happy. He finally had the family he had always dreamed of having.

21

Ben reached for the edge of Anna's shirt to pull it over her head.

"No, wait. Stop," she said.

It was all happening too fast.

"Is something wrong?" asked Ben.

"I'm sorry, please forgive me. I just got caught up in the moment," he said with sincerity.

"It's not that. . ." She broke down and told him about the baby. She didn't see how this could possibly work out with her pregnant and being on vacation. She was near tears talking to him.

"I really like you. . .it's just my life is a mess," she cried.

Ben started laughing. She looked at him like he was crazy.

"Why are you laughing?" she asked.

"Your life's not a mess. You just make bad decisions. Look at you – you're beautiful, talented, have a baby on the way. You've got lots of things going for you," he said.

She decided Ben must be the craziest man she had ever met.

"If you want to make excuses why we can't be

together, you can do that, but they're your excuses," Ben replied.

Anna wasn't sure what to make of him or any of this for that matter. She asked if she could go home for a while to think. He drove her back to the cottage, gave her his phone number and told her to call him when she was ready.

The next couple of days Anna sat on the beach staring at her cell phone, almost pressing the numbers and then deciding against it. She got out her bikini, slathered herself down with suntan lotion and tried to forget about this crazy man that she had just met. She just met him. Her life was in shambles. It just wasn't meant to be.

She thought about her vision from the other day and how Ben seemed to fit right into it. *Argh, she had come to the beach to straighten things out and now they were in even more of a tangle.* What was she going to tell Midge when she got back? She tried to push Ben out of her mind by turning up her iPod. She sang "Girls Just Wanna Have Fun" to the baby as she rubbed her belly.

She couldn't stay here. She didn't have a job. Besides, why would some man she just met want a pregnant woman as a girlfriend? *There must be something wrong with him. He must have some type of hidden mental illness or something.*

Anna came in from the beach, dusted the sand off of her feet and took a shower. She wrapped herself in a towel and lay down on the bed. She noticed Jacob's diary on the nightstand. She thought about Jacob and Helen. *That was kind of a crazy situation too, wasn't it? I mean her crazy husband wanted to kill him and her both and then they ended up together? That was way more screwed up than her and Ben.* She pushed at her self-doubt. Maybe if she actually believed that things were possible, that everything could work out – then maybe they would. It seemed a crazy thought. But, all of the "rational" thoughts she had had up to this point hadn't done her much good. *What was she staying in Cincinnati for anyway? There was nothing to stay there for anymore.* But, where would she find a job at the beach?

She got dressed in Capri pants and a blouse and walked down to a local Mexican restaurant. She ate her chicken taco with rice and beans and felt pangs of sorrow tugging at her heart. She was so close to having everything she wanted and yet here she was eating tacos by herself.

On the way out the door, she picked up the local paper and took it home to the cottage. She tossed it in her suitcase as a souvenir of her time here and then walked out onto the beach to collect shells. She wrote Ben a note explaining that she had to leave tomorrow, but she had enjoyed their time together so much and wished things could have worked out. Anna drove over to Ben's house and slipped the note under the mat. When she got home, she took a long walk on the beach, promised herself she would eat better and then went home to sleep.

The next morning there was a knock on the door. It was Ben. She was still in her pajamas and a bit embarrassed by her appearance, but she opened the door anyway.

"Look, I respect your decision. If you believe we can't be together, then we can't be together. But, I wanted to kiss you goodbye," he said.

Anna looked at him with tears in her eyes and kissed him for a few minutes. She said, "Goodbye," pulled away and shut the door and then burst into tears.

Anna packed up her toiletries, pulled her clothes out of the drawers and said goodbye to the little cottage. She took one last walk on the beach and then got in the car. She felt heartbroken but told herself it was all for the best.

The drive back toward Cincinnati felt long and sorrowful. The mountains seemed to symbolize the insurmountable obstacles she faced. She had no idea what she was going to tell Midge when she got home. Anna thought about stopping but mostly just wanted the ride to be over, to return to her comfort zone and the way things were and always had been.

When she arrived at Midge's house, Midge walked out

to greet her and help her with her bag. It was late and Midge realized she was probably exhausted.

"How was your trip?" she asked cheerfully.

Anna started to cry and ran to her room. Midge left her alone to sleep off her trip and deal with whatever she was dealing with. Anna came out in the morning and told Midge all about her trip and Ben.

Midge said, "It's a shame you can't find a job out there, honey. That boy sounds perfect for you."

"You think?" said Anna.

She perked up, glad to have Midge's approval, but then realized she had to go in and face Brad today.

"Midge, can we drive in together? I don't think I can face Brad alone," Anna asked.

"Sure thing, just let me get some coffee in me first," said Midge.

She poured herself a cup and took it to her bedroom to get ready. Work boots on, Midge walked out with Anna to the cars to face the music.

As they walked in the building, Anna walked straight toward Brad while Midge went to her position in line.

Brad fumed at Anna, "Voicemail, Perrault? Seriously? Where's this medical documentation? You cannot just take a week off work without medical documentation! I'm surprised you would even show your face in this building. This is the last straw. You better have brought some paperwork with you."

Anna bit her tongue and tried not to retaliate.

"Brad, I'd appreciate it if you would not yell at me in front of the staff. Can we talk in private?" she seethed between her teeth.

"No, Perrault. If you have something to say you can say it here and now in front of the staff. They're the ones that have to pick up your slack when you decide not to show up for work. So, let's hear it," said Brad.

"I'm pregnant and I wasn't feeling well," said Anna.

"Pregnant? I feel sorry for that child. Well, you and I

both know we can't have a pregnant woman on the floor, so I guess you'll be requesting leave. Good luck getting your job back when you return" said Brad.

Anna had been practicing breathing the whole time that Brad spoke, but her anger raged inside of her. She was so tired of being pushed around by this little tyrant.

"I don't want the job back, Brad. I came in to tell you I quit and not because I'm pregnant. I'm quitting because you're an asshole, this job sucks and I can't stand one more minute of your condescending bullshit. You parade around this warehouse like you're the King of England. Well, you're not Brad. It's a warehouse. We put crap in boxes. It doesn't mean anything. And I want more than that," yelled Anna.

"Good luck getting another job with the reference I'm going to give you, missy! This "crappy" job pays your bills. Another single mom on welfare – wow, you're a real winner Perrault. You're right. You deserve exactly what you get!" screamed Brad.

Anna walked out shrugging her shoulders at Midge as she walked by her on the floor.

Anna got in her car and slammed the door. God, she hated Brad. She was so happy to never have to see him again. She had no idea what she was going to do, but at least she wouldn't have to see Brad's face again. She slammed her fist against the steering wheel a few times.

She went toward Midge's house driving a little too fast. She sat in the driveway for a while crying, feeling like she had let Midge down. Where was she going to go now? She went in the house and crawled under the covers, wanting to hide from the world and everyone in it. She laid there, a hysterical crying mess until Midge got home.

"That Brad," Midge fumed. "Why if I didn't need that job, I'd tell him to stick it where the sun don't shine. Good for you standing up to him. Boy was he pissed. He yelled at everybody the whole damn day!" said Midge.

"I'm so sorry, Midge. I'm such an awful friend. You

give me a place to stay and I get knocked up, quit my job and stay with you for months. I take your money and go on vacation and come back no better off than when I left. With friends like me, who needs enemies?" said Anna.

"Now sugar, you're just going through a bad spell. Old Midge knows your heart and she knows you have a good heart. Everything's going to turn around. You'll see. You just got to believe it will," said Midge.

"I'm trying Midge, I'm trying," said Anna.

22

Jacob cut the ribbon and proclaimed the St. Joseph Orphanage open for business. Reporters took photographs and asked for interviews. A crowd clamored around Jacob and his friends as Sister Catherine arrived with the orphans beside her to enter their new home for the very first time. Jacob walked in behind them and watched the children shout with joy at the sight of their new beds. Several of them ran over to hug him. Jacob looked around for Helen to share his excitement.

Jacob had seen a lot of Helen these last six months. They had gone out on the town twice, once to the play and once to the circus. They had been at each other's houses for dinner a couple of nights a week. Now, he would get to see her every time he checked in on the orphanage. He saw in each and every face Molly's face and felt he had really done a good thing for these kids and the community by completing the project.

He had been so busy with Helen, the orphanage and his business affairs that he had been missing some meetings at the Masonic Lodge. He felt guilty about that and promised himself he would go to the meeting that evening and apologize for his absence of late.

Just then, he spotted Helen behind a mob of children. He carefully moved past the herd to get to her in the back.

"Are you sure you're ready to feed all these little ones?" asked Jacob.

"I'll do my best," said Helen.

He wrapped his arm around her waist and they smiled at the children and their glee at their new surroundings. Sister Catherine came over and reached her hand out to Helen.

"You must be Helen, our new cook. Mr. Hoffner has many kind things to say about you," said Sister Catherine.

"I've heard many kind words about you as well, Sister Catherine," said Helen.

"Let me show you to the kitchen, Helen. If you'll excuse us, Mr. Hoffner," said Sister Catherine taking Helen by the arm and leading her out of the room.

Jacob stepped aside to let them pass. He stayed the remainder of the day playing with the children and helping them unpack their things. Helen served their first meal in the new house and they both sat and enjoyed the vegetable soup and sandwiches. Then Helen and Jacob left Sister Catherine to take over for the remainder of the evening. Jacob walked Helen home, kissed her goodnight and headed off to the Masonic lodge.

He had heard the Grandmaster was thinking of retiring. He had been in poor health and was having difficulty standing during the long induction ceremonies. Entering through the heavy oak door, he hoped his brethren weren't too displeased with him for being absent of late. When he walked into the room full of men, he was surprised to see a dessert buffet set up. *Was there some kind of party tonight?* Henry greeted him in a warm embrace. Matthew patted him on the back. Men rushed forward to shake his hand. The Grandmaster called the meeting to order.

"I now call to order this meeting. In honor of the opening of St. Joseph Orphanage, we gather together tonight to congratulate our brother, Jacob Hoffner on a job well done. Let us raise our glasses in a toast. To Mr. Hoffner," he said raising his glass in the air.

Jacob was surprised by the warm reception and very touched. He milled about the room, catching up, laughing and joining in conversations. Everyone seemed to be in good spirits. Even those men, who had sided with Wayne during his lifetime, seemed to have let all of that go and spoke to him like they were old friends. While Jacob served himself a slice of peach pie, Cecil came by to congratulate him.

"There's talk that you'll be voted in as the next Grandmaster, Jacob. I don't think you have any opposition."

Jacob smiled at the news. He had not aspired to such a high position, but was flattered that the others would want him to take it. Nicholas Brundy had done a good job the last 20 years in the role and those would be tough shoes to fill.

Jacob left that night feeling like everything was going his way. His business was thriving, the orphanage had just opened, he was about to be named Grandmaster and he had a beautiful girlfriend and family. A year ago, Jacob would have never believed this possible. Yet, somewhere inside he must have had a feeling that everything would work out. It all seemed destined somehow.

There was only one thing missing that would make life all the better. The next morning he went to the jeweler to buy a ring. He chose a simple diamond surrounded by five hearts, a heart to symbolize each one of the children that would comprise their new family. He invited Helen out for a picnic in the park since it was supposed to be a beautiful day. Helen smiled as Jacob smoothed out the blanket, laid out the sandwiches and salad.

"Jacob, you went to so much trouble, what's the occasion?" she asked.

"I'm just happy. I want to celebrate your new job, the

orphanage, us. . ." Helen smiled while Jacob poured her a glass of wine.

"There's also one more thing I would like to celebrate," Jacob said and then waited with a long dramatic pause.

"What's that?" Helen asked.

Jacob got down on one knee, took Helen's hand and asked "Will you marry me?"

Tears fell from Helen's eyes.

"Yes, oh yes. Nothing would make me happier," she exclaimed.

Jacob leaned forward to kiss her.

"Would you like to come over for dinner tonight and we could tell the children then?" Jacob asked.

"That sounds like a perfect idea," said Helen.

They enjoyed the rest of the hour, smiling and kissing between bites of sandwich. Then Helen hurried off to help out at the orphanage and Jacob went off to the office.

A little past 6:00, the boys arrived with Helen. They had quizzical looks on their faces. They expected that something was going on, but had no idea what it could be.

Molly opened the door and shouted, "Papa, the boys are here!"

She had already begun to regard them as brothers. Jacob had made a special dinner for the occasion. He set the roast on the table, along with the potatoes and carrots. He asked Molly to get the drinks and set out the napkins and silverware. When they were all seated, Jacob smiled and looked at each of the children.

"Boys, your mother and I have something to tell you. We're going to be married."

Molly squealed, "Oh Papa, really! We're all going to be a family!" The boys all had smiles on their faces, except William, the oldest. He seemed to be the most protective of his mother.

"Are you sure? You haven't been dating that long," he said.

"I assure you that I love your mother very much and will treat her with respect as long as I live," said Jacob.

His response seemed to satisfy the boy and they all ate their meals in happy silence. As they cleared the dishes, there was much talk of moving and living arrangements. There were two spare rooms upstairs and Jacob said he would make arrangements for two boys each to share a room. Molly seemed happy to be a girl since she was the only one who got to have a room to herself.

Jacob and Helen were married on a Saturday in July. They married in the gardens out back by the pond. Helen wore a simple white cotton dress with a lace overlay and had a small veil covering her face. She carried white roses. The boys acted as best men. Molly was the maid of honor and shone in a peach taffeta gown with roses in her hair. Jacob stood with pride and joy as his new wife came down the aisle, so blessed to have found love again at his age.

The couple soon became the talk of the town, with Jacob the Grandmaster and Helen the head cook at the orphanage. Jacob gathered the Masons together for several fundraisers, often inviting people over for parties at their home. Helen would cook and the children would help out. They raised hundreds of dollars for local schools, charities, and churches. But, the orphanage remained closest to Jacob's heart because he often thought of how proud he was of Molly and the woman she was becoming.

They had been married a few years, when Henry Marsden once again brought up the idea of a trip to Europe.

"I'm beginning to believe you're a load of hot air, Jacob. I've been trying to get you to go overseas for years and you keep putting me off. You're entirely too busy old man. It's time you took that family of yours on a vacation."

And for once, Jacob agreed. The children were getting older and seemed capable of withstanding the long voyage and even the youngest, George, seemed like he would be old enough to remember the trip. There were a few last certifications Jacob wanted to acquire for his Mason degrees. But, he wanted to go most of all because Helen had never been overseas and he wanted to show her the land where her ancestors came from and all the magnificent sights he had seen when he had last been.

So, Jacob took leave from work and packed up trunks full of clothing for the family. They were to travel by train to the East Coast and then board a boat for London. Molly was 12 now and had taken to mothering the little ones, so she helped George onto the train and held his little hand as he seemed frightened by the loud roar of the engine. The children couldn't stop staring out of the windows as the train pulled away from the station. They had never traveled so far and seemed to have a newfound respect for Jacob and all of his knowledge about foreign lands.

As they traveled, Jacob told them tales of his youth – riding gondolas in Venice, learning baking techniques from the Parisians and touring the castles of England. As night fell, he told tales of torture and terror about the Tower of London as the children nestled together nervously staring out at the black landscape passing beside them through the train windows.

When they finally arrived in Massachusetts, the children seemed a bit worn out, so Jacob took them down to the ocean to play for a bit before boarding the boat. The children had never seen the ocean and were spellbound by it. He almost couldn't pull them away from it to board the ship.

"I always thought Cincinnati was so big, Papa. But, the ocean makes me feel so small. The world is huge, Papa. It's like we're little tiny stars in a huge sky," said Molly.

Jacob agreed and said she hadn't seen anything yet.

The boat was large and luxurious. They were lucky enough to acquire first class cabins. The children had their own room complete with bunk beds and were making the most of it. For the most part, Helen and he let the children run about the decks for a while, and they tried to rest in the cabin. He was beginning to think he was too old for intercontinental travel. It had been much easier when he was a young man. But, the children's excitement was contagious and in no time, he felt revived and joined them on deck to play some shuffleboard.

When they arrived in London, a representative from the Masonic Order greeted Jacob at the ship and took the family in his carriage to their hotel. Jacob would spend his weekdays training for his final certifications. He had evenings and weekends free to spend with the children. Helen took them sightseeing to Buckingham Palace, the Tower of London, Westminster Abbey and Stratford-upon-Avon.

When Jacob returned in the evening, Molly would excitedly tell him about the day's adventure and ask what he had planned for the weekend. He couldn't discuss much about his training as he was sworn to secrecy by Masonic code, but he explained that mainly what he was learning was that it was his job as Grandmaster to shine a light into their community and make the place they lived a place where everyone wanted to be.

Finally, Saturday arrived and Jacob took Molly to the one place where she had begging to go with him. Molly had been learning a lot in school about ancient sites and the origins of civilization. She devoured learning anything about history and had been telling Helen tidbits about the history of England the entire week. So, when Jacob told her he was taking her to Stonehenge, she was beside herself with excitement. Henry had taken Jacob there on their last trip, so he picked them up and drove them out to the site.

When Molly stepped off the carriage onto the lush green hill misted in fog, a change came over her. Jacob could not describe it or explain it but he could feel something different about Molly. She walked up to each of the large stone columns and touched them. She stood in the center and seemed to go into a type of trance.

It was then that Jacob noticed what it was that was changed. Molly seemed to have a glow about her, a bright light that emanated from her body. He had always known Molly was special but for the first time he realized that Molly wasn't just figuratively an angel, it seemed she truly was one.

"What's the matter, Papa?" she asked glowing atop the green hill.

"It's nothing, Molly. You just look especially beautiful today."

Their conversation turned to history and how and when these monuments could have been placed there. It was a miracle they even found the place, but Henry had connections at the museum who had given him a map to the location. They sat for a while in that sacred space and let the feeling of it sink in. Jacob wondered what Molly's future would hold. He felt very deeply, that her presence in his life was not a coincidence, but destiny.

23

Anna dragged around for days, reading magazines on the couch while Midge was at work. She tried helping out by making dinner. She looked in the newspaper daily for jobs. She missed Ben terribly. At long last, out of boredom, she decided to continue reading Jacob's diary. But, she got frustrated when she read of his happiness. It was too much to take when she was in the height of despair. She decided what she really needed was to talk to Jacob again, so she banged away at her laptop trying desperately to finish the novel, so she could at least do one thing right in her life.

She thought about going to visit him before she finished the novel, but he had said he wouldn't speak with her until the draft was complete. And she couldn't bear the idea of going there only to be faced with solitude and isolation. She laughed to herself and thought that was funny since that was the reason she started visiting that gravesite in the first place.

Her clothes were starting to get too tight. She found herself unbuttoning the top of her pants and trying to cover the opening up with a long shirt. She took her prenatal vitamins and tried to eat her vegetables. She took long walks outside. She even went back to the yoga class at the Hoffner Lodge a few times. The doctor said she was progressing well and that she could find out on her next visit the sex of the baby.

She wondered what Ben was doing now, if he had moved on to some other girl. He was better off without her. Still, she couldn't escape the feeling that they were meant to be. There had been all those coincidences. She had been so distraught these last few weeks that she hadn't even unpacked her suitcase from her trip.

So, one Tuesday, while trying to tidy up the place for Midge, she decided to finally pull her clothes out of her suitcase and throw them in the laundry. As she carried handfuls of the dirty shorts and swimsuits to the washer, she noticed the newspaper rolled up in the corner of the suitcase. She had forgotten buying it. She flopped down on the bed, opened it and scanned the articles. It was a beach town, so there were stories about pollution, warnings about high tides and sea turtle sightings. She perused the items for sale, beach umbrellas, old patio furniture, used golf carts. She turned the page to the jobs section. There was an opening for a lifeguard, several server positions at local restaurants. . .and then one particular opening caught her eye. It was for a public relations position at a local children's home. They wanted an entry level person who could write grants, who cared about children and would be willing to work weekend charity events.

Her breath caught. It was the perfect job. It was exactly what she wanted. Ben had told her to believe, that if she believed then things would work out. And she hadn't believed him. But, there, in black and white was the job she had been dreaming about all of her life. Was it too late? She wrote down the email address and hurried over to her laptop. She emailed the contact person to ask if the position was still available and expressed her interest in the job.

She paced around the house in a tizzy. The

newspaper was weeks old. Someone might have accepted the position already. Should she just go there? But, she had a doctor's appointment in two weeks! She couldn't leave now. Maybe they could move up the doctor's appointment. She grabbed her cell phone and frantically called the doctor. Dr. Wheeler said she could get her scheduled in one week for the ultrasound. That was a little better.

When Midge got home, Anna practically tackled her to tell her the news.

"Midge, you'll never believe what happened!" she said, slightly shaking the old woman.

"Calm down, girl," Midge said. "Help me get these groceries inside and tell me all about it," said Midge.

Anna told her about the job ad and the ultrasound.

"Now, don't go and count your chickens before they're hatched," said Midge. "You don't even know if this job is still available yet. But, I like seeing you excited. I never once saw that look on your face when you thought about going into the warehouse," said Midge. "Are you going to call Ben?"

"No, not yet," said Anna. "I want to see if this is a possibility. I know I was stupid to leave and I know he probably would've let me stay with him without a job. But, I want to feel like a whole person, a person with purpose. I don't want to be a down on her luck woman with a baby. I want to be a confident woman who gives something to the relationship and doesn't just take from it. Does that make sense?" said Anna.

"I hear ya," said Midge. "Well, I guess you'll just have to wait and see if they email you back."

For the next two days, Anna hit refresh on her computer about a million times. She cleaned every inch of Midge's house in an attempt to keep her mind off of it. Finally, an email from the Outer Banks Children's Home arrived in her inbox. It said that they had interviewed a few candidates but had not found the right fit and were reopening the posting. If she would like to be considered, they would welcome a cover letter and resume. They also wanted to see a short writing sample.

Anna began typing the letter. She explained that she was only starting out as a writer, but was eager to learn. For her writing sample, she included a portion of Jacob's novel that talked about his love for the orphanage and the children there. She hit send and hoped for the best.

Days passed and there was no response. Anna began to worry. But, today, she had other things on her mind. She was finally going in for the ultrasound. She put on her maternity blouse that Midge had purchased for her, as she was now too big for her own clothing and drove herself to the doctor's office. This visit wasn't as anxiety filled as the others. She felt excited to find out the sex of the baby and wondered if the Indian man's prediction was right. She followed the nurse back to the ultrasound technician and lay down on the chair. The technician squeezed the cold jelly on her stomach and rubbed it around.

"Let's see what we have here," said the technician.

An image popped up on the computer. Anna could see a head and a body but really couldn't make out much else about the baby.

"Would you like to know the sex?" asked the technician.

"Yes," said Anna.

"Well, it looks like you're going to have a little girl," said the technician.

"Are you sure?" asked Anna.

"Pretty sure, it's not always 100% accurate, but she's not being shy, and I don't see anything down there, so I'm pretty sure it's a girl," said the technician.

Anna felt a burst of joy and love ripple through her. She would have to think of a name. She rubbed her belly and thought, "Hello, little girl."

All the way home, Anna smiled and couldn't wait to tell Midge the news. She went through names in her head and tried them out with Perrault. She wasn't having much luck, so she went to the baby naming sites on the internet when she got home to look up meanings. She wanted a name that meant something good or lucky. She could use that in her life right now and she wanted that for her daughter. Gwyneth – no, Hillary – no, Felicia – no. She liked Bella but didn't want to name her baby after a character from *Twilight*. She settled on Callie for the moment. It meant beautiful and she liked the way it sounded. She sat her head down on the bed, exhausted from surfing the internet. Just then, her inbox pinged. She had another email from the children's home! She couldn't believe her eyes! They wanted her to come in for an interview and the director asked that she call her in the morning.

Anna picked up the phone to call Ben and then put it down again. She couldn't try to reconcile over the phone. She needed to see him in person. Anna was going to drive out for the interview anyway, so she would see him then. She laid her head back on the pillow and tried to breathe deeply. She was filled with both excitement and fear. She tried to push the negative thoughts from her mind.

Everything is going to be alright, she said to herself over and over. It became her mantra and lulled her to sleep.

The next morning she called the children's home and asked for Elaine Downey, the director. Elaine got on the phone, told Anna a little about the history of the children's home. It was founded in 1932 and they served 350 children each year. Funding had been cut in recent years and they were in dire need of a grant writer who could improve the living conditions at the facility. They couldn't pay a large salary, so they were looking for someone who would be willing to take an entry level position at first with raises possible in the future. They had good medical and dental benefits.

"When would you be available for an interview, Ms. Perrault?" asked Elaine.

"I can come on Friday," Anna replied realizing that meant she would need to spend all of the next day driving.

"I'll see at 10:00 a.m. on Friday," said Elaine.

As Anna hung up the phone, she had a good feeling. She felt like it might just be possible that she would get the job. She just hoped she hadn't royally screwed things up with Ben. *Why was she so stupid?*

The next day she packed and hugged Midge goodbye. Anna insisted she could sleep in her car because she wasn't taking another dime from Midge, but Midge wouldn't hear of it. She wasn't having her godchild sleep in a car. Midge handed her a wad of cash, kissed her on the cheek and wished her good luck. Anna constantly had to check the speedometer as she drove, realizing at times she seemed to be racing toward the mountains.

While the last time she drove out there she was filled with uncertainty, this time she was driven by purpose and sheer determination. She maneuvered the curves with ease and made it the full 10 hours by nightfall. It was too short of notice to secure a cottage, and she thought it would stir up sad memories. So, she acquired modest accommodations at a Red Roof Inn near the outskirts of town.

There was no ocean view to distract her, but she could still smell the salty air when she stepped out onto the balcony. She sat on the hotel bed and practiced her answers to possible interview questions, ironed the suit she had brought with her and hoped her obvious pregnancy wasn't going to work against her. She called the front desk for a wakeup call, went to bed early and tried to will herself to get some rest for her big day. But, she tossed and turned, both uncomfortable in her condition and too nervous to sleep.

The sunlight hit her eyes through the blinds before the wakeup call came. At first, she felt disoriented, forgetting where she was and grappling for the light on the nightstand. She went to ready herself in the bathroom and must have checked her teeth for lipstick five times in the mirror. She was too nervous to eat, so she simply ate an apple she purchased from the lobby convenience store, had some decaf coffee and was on her way.

The children's home was in the downtown area a few miles from the beach. If you could call it a downtown, it seemed to have enjoyed its heyday in the 1950s and declined since that era. But, there were some cute independent shops mostly catering to tourists in the area. She parked at a meter and walked down the street to 342 Main St, the address that Elaine had given her. It was an older building but seemed to be well taken care of. There was a colorful mural painted on the outside of a rainbow and children playing. The words Outer Banks Children's Home hung above the door in bubble letters.

A bell chimed as Anna entered the blue door. She checked in at the reception area and sat nervously on a hard plastic seat in the waiting room for Elaine to come out and meet her. Elaine emerged from a back room. She looked to be about 45 years old, with auburn hair styled in a bob. She seemed very animated and wore a lot of makeup but also had sort of a cool bohemian vibe to her. She wore a bright artistic scarf and handcrafted bangles on her wrists. She greeted Anna warmly and invited her back to her office. There were two other board members present for the interview. Anna shook the hands of a tall, bald gentleman with a persistent grin on his face and a short, brunette who looked very young, but was full of enthusiasm.

Anna nervously sat at the end of the table and awaited their questions. To her surprise, they didn't seem overly concerned by her lack of experience, but seemed more concerned about whether she would get along with the staff and be a good fit. She felt instantly at ease with the people at the table and to her surprise seemed to answer the interview questions with a sense of ease and confidence. They didn't inquire about the pregnancy, but suggested that she would be able to do some work from home if coming in every day was a concern. She was still uncertain about whether she actually had the job when Elaine remarked on her writing sample.

"What impressed us most, Ms. Perrault, was the writing sample you sent. Is it something you wrote for a magazine?" she asked.

"Oh no, I've been writing a novel," Anna explained.

She told them the overall plot and they seemed impressed with her dedication to the project.

"The way you describe the care and attitude of the staff toward the children in your novel is very similar to the atmosphere we have here, Ms. Perrault. It was like you could see into our little place and what makes it special. It was that writing sample that made us feel your employment here was simply meant to be. We would be happy to offer you the position if you want it," said Elaine smiling.

Anna was overjoyed, gave an enthusiastic yes and vigorously shook the hands of the two board members and Elaine. She explained that she would have to make moving arrangements but could start within the month. Everyone seemed to find that agreeable, offered to help in any way they could and asked her to call when she was all settled in to her new place. Anna walked out the doors onto the busy street and made her way to her car. She sat for a moment realizing there was only one thing left to do. She had to see Ben and she had to see him right now.

She drove toward the beach, the familiar sights coming in to view. She passed the boardwalk, the grocery; she stopped in front of the cottage and reminisced about her time there. She drove slowly toward Ben's house, not sure if he would be home or if he would be alone. She hoped and prayed that he would be. When she arrived, she noticed his car wasn't in the driveway. She circled the block a few times, got out and tried to peer in the windows. He wasn't home. So, she drove back down toward the boardwalk and parked the car.

She got out and took her shoes and pantyhose off. She felt a little ridiculous being on the beach in a suit, but the cool sand felt good in between her toes. She walked down toward the edge of the ocean and picked up a stick. She wrote "I love Ben" in the sand and then went to sit on the boardwalk and stare out at the waves.

She stared at the sunlight glimmering on the waves and tried to consciously bring the light inside of her. The sun felt warm against her closed eyelids. Everything was coming together. *Please, Ben, please forgive me*, she thought. She realized she hadn't eaten anything except an apple since that morning so she walked back toward the food court and ordered a hamburger. She sat on a nearby picnic table, squeezing ketchup and mustard onto the bun. She took off her suit coat and let the sun warm her shoulders. She heard someone come up behind her.

"Hey stranger," said the man.

He sat down beside her. She turned to see Ben wearing shorts and another Thoreau t-shirt (this time with a saying about marching to the beat of your own drummer).

"Hey," she said.

She had practiced a speech the entire drive down, but now felt dumbfounded to see him sitting there beside her.

"What are you doing here?" Ben asked. "And why are you wearing a suit on the beach?" he asked wiping a bit of ketchup off of her cheek.

Anna started to launch into the story about the children's home job, but paused for a moment and stared into Ben's eyes.

"I miss you. I couldn't stop thinking about you. I tried. I told myself you were better off without me. But, it didn't work. When I was with you I felt like I was home – like this place was more my home than where I grew up had ever been. There was this empty place inside of me that disappeared in your presence. And when I left you, it grew. A couple of weeks ago I found a newspaper that I bought when I was here and while reading it, I came across the perfect writing job. So, I had to come back and see – see if this wonderful life I'd envisioned out on the beach was a real possibility. I'm sorry I left. Can you forgive me?" asked Anna.

Ben brushed some hair out of Anna's eyes that was whipping about in the wind.

"I could see when we were here that you didn't believe in yourself. That's why I didn't chase after you. But, I always believed in you, believed in us. You've changed. I can see it in your eyes. You believe it too, now. And now you're here and I couldn't be happier. I missed you too," said Ben.

"So, it's not too late?" asked Anna.

Ben laughed, "No, it's not too late."

Anna proceeded to tell him all about the interview and the job offer. He hugged her and offered his congratulations.

"How's the baby?" he asked.

"It's a girl. The Indian man was right. I've decided to name her Callie. It means beautiful," said Anna. "I haven't thought of a middle name yet. Do you have any ideas?"

"How about Callie Angelina – Beautiful Angel – like her mother?"

"I love that," said Anna.

"Would you like to go back to my place and talk for a while?" asked Ben.

Anna agreed. They got up, threw the food wrappers away and she hopped in Ben's car. Ben talked to her on the way about how he had kept busy with work and spent a lot of nights thinking about her, hoping she would return. Anna smiled.

As they entered through the front door, Anna looked around and imagined her life in this place. She looked through the glass patio doors and saw herself writing overlooking the ocean. She looked at the couch and pictured herself and Ben watching movies together. She looked at the kitchen and saw the two of them chopping vegetables and cooking. It felt like home. And a few minutes later, it was Ben who asked her to move in with him.

"I understand if you would rather live on your own for a while. I know this is all really fast," said Ben.

"I don't want to rush you. I can find you an inexpensive apartment near your new job if you would like," he said.

"No, I want to be here, with you," said Anna.

For once in her life, she didn't want to run away from anything, she wanted to run towards something. She explained to Ben that the new job started in a month and she would need to go home and pack up her things.

"Would you like me to go with you?" he asked.

"No, I need to do this one last thing myself," said Anna.

She decided to stay a couple of days and then leave on the day long trip back to Cincinnati.

"How about I take you on a proper date before you go back?" said Ben.

"Where are you taking me?" she asked.

"It's a surprise. You rest up; get yourself out of that suit. Watch some TV. I'm going to go out for a while. I have an appointment to show a house and then I'll be back to get you," said Ben.

"O.K." said Anna and gave him a long kiss goodbye.

When he left, she spent a few minutes being nosy. She opened the cabinets and the refrigerator to see what kind of food he ate. She found mostly organic vegetables, lots of fruit, some steaks. She found a stash of dark chocolate on top of the refrigerator and popped a few pieces into her mouth. She looked at his collection of movies and read the titles of his books. There were some guy action flicks, the entire *Die Hard* Trilogy, but also some movies she liked like *Good Will Hunting* and *The Breakfast*

Club.

He had several real estate books, a lot of Thoreau and Emerson, books on surfing and a few historical fiction novels. Anna wanted to learn everything she could about this man who had enchanted her. She finally realized she was exhausted, set the alarm on her cell phone and took a nap on the couch.

Thirty minutes before Ben was to return, she got ready for their date. She curled her hair, put on makeup and slipped on a little black maternity dress which she had found at the thrift store in good condition. She surveyed her appearance in the mirror – not too shabby. Ben returned with roses in his hand which set on the kitchen table.

"My lady, shall we?" he said taking her hand.

They drove up the coast into the mountains. The drive took nearly an hour, but when they stopped at the little restaurant on the cliff, Anna was awestruck. It was a tiny restaurant, adorned in twinkling lights and nestled into the hillside. The terrain was rocky and Ben took her hand to make sure she wouldn't slip on the way down to the entrance. The waiters were dressed in white jackets and a jazz singer stood in the corner singing ballads backed up by a piano player and a man on saxophone. Their table was by the window. Ben pulled out her seat for her to sit down.

"This is where the sea lions like to play," Ben said pointing out to the rocks below.

She could see them out there rolling around on top of each other and splashing in the water. She smiled.

"It's wonderful, Ben. It really is," she said.

He ordered some sparkling cider and raised his glass in a toast.

"To your new job as a writer, Anna Perrault. And to us and our new family," said Ben.

"I'll toast to that," said Anna.

They sat dining on Italian pasta, salad and tiramisu as

the sun set over the ocean. Anna had never been happier. When they returned home, she slept in his arms and felt safe and sound and peaceful. They spent the next day walking on the beach, talking for hours and laughing. Ben was so funny and she couldn't stop smiling.

Finally, the time came for her to drive back to Cincinnati.

"I can't wait until you get back. Are you sure you don't want me to go with you?" asked Ben.

"I'll be fine. I called Midge. She's going to get some friends of hers to help me load the U-Haul. So, I'll just need some help unloading when I get here."

Ben kept reaching out to hug her as she inched her way towards the door. He was afraid she might disappear again. Anna had a hard time letting go too, but knew she had some unfinished business. She was more determined than ever to finish this novel and start the next chapter of her life.

24

The next day, Henry picked up Jacob from the hotel and they made their way to the Masonic Lodge of London. Jacob was still thinking about the light he had seen around Molly the day before and was wondering what it could mean. They gave the password and the secret sign and entered the large doors.

Jacob was impressed by the grandeur of the place. Their membership was in the hundreds and spanned centuries. Large chandeliers hung in the entry, the floors were a deep cherry hardwood covered by intricately designed Persian carpets. The Grandmaster of the London Lodge, Jeremiah Harrington, was in his eighties and had a sage like quality about himself.

Jacob mingled with the other men before they began the training. He had met some of them before in his travels abroad and they caught up on news of marriages and children born. Henry had been there several times over the years and introduced Jacob to some newer members of the Order.

The rituals began and Jacob was even more mesmerized than he was at home in his own lodge. There was something about the recitation of the ancient teachings in this foreign land with hundreds of men that felt powerful. Jacob felt he was coming into contact with a universal consciousness which he had previously not been able to touch.

When they had finished for the day, Jacob felt spent and exhausted but somehow renewed as if his life force had been amplified. He asked Jeremiah if he could speak with him for a moment. Jeremiah asked for a few moments to put books and adornments away while Jacob waited patiently in the alcove of the stairs. He then followed Jeremiah up the spiral staircase to his study. Jacob gazed around the room at the multitude of books lining the wall. It seemed almost more of a library than a study. Jeremiah lit the lamp on the desktop and motioned for Jacob to have a seat.

"What can I do for you, Mr. Hoffner?" he asked.

Jacob told him about his trip to Stonehenge and the strange glow he had seen around Molly.

"What do you think it means, Grandmaster?" asked Jacob.

"You are familiar with our concept of the Masonic light, are you not, Mr. Hoffner?" said Jeremiah.

"Yes, of course, it has been my guiding force for almost fifty years," said Jacob.

"Well, it is said, that there are those among us that are angels in human form. They are sent to help us, indeed to help humanity. They are usually very compassionate, loving souls that make others better in their presence. It is said that these individuals possess a glow which can be seen in sacred spaces," said Jeremiah.

"But, what does this mean for my Molly and her future?" asked Jacob.

"It means that she will do great good in this world and that, in the afterlife, she will become one of those great golden orbs in the sky. Her progeny will live in the light and likewise, have the potential to bring great light into this world," said Jeremiah.

"Why has she come to me?" asked Jacob.

"I have heard of your great kindness and generosity, the great good you have done for your community through your orphanage and the fundraising you've done for schools. As Grandmaster of your lodge, you are the protector of the light. Molly is the light that has come to you, and your job is to protect her and her legacy for future generations," said Jeremiah.

Jacob thanked the Grandmaster for his time and insight and went downstairs where Henry was waiting to take him to the hotel.

Jacob began to think of all his interactions with Molly since the beginning – the way she had cheered him up and prevented his suicide after Elizabeth died, the way when she came to live with him she made his world whole again, the way she sparkled in her fairy wings and how she had taken Helen's boys under her wing as if they had been members of the family all along.

He smiled as he returned to the hotel and walked through the lobby doors. Jacob felt like a man truly blessed. When he got back to the room, he found William and the boys playing cards and Molly with her nose in a book. Helen was sitting on the bed sewing a new dress.

"How would the lot of you like to go out to spend the day on the shore of Lake Windermere tomorrow?" asked Jacob.

"That sounds fun," said William. "Isn't that where Wordsworth and the other Lake Poets live?" asked Molly. Molly shared his love of Thoreau, Wordsworth and the other Romantics.

"One and the same," said Jacob.

"A most excellent idea, Papa," said Molly returning to her book.

They spent their evening relaxing in the room. Jacob joined the boys in their card game and let them win a hand or two.

The next morning Jacob got everyone up bright and

early to make the trek out to Lake Windermere. They put on the warmest clothes they had brought with them. Jacob had forgotten how much chillier England could be. But, it was still a pleasant day and they packed a picnic lunch and brought along fishing rods.

When they arrived, they set out blankets and Molly went with the boys to fish down by the shore. Jacob took the opportunity to steal a kiss from Helen. He didn't mind the fine lines forming about her eyes; she looked as beautiful as ever to him. They enjoyed their alone time, talking as much about his certifications as the secret code would allow. Jacob skipped over the part about Molly, never wanting Helen to feel like she was favored over the other children.

"Do you ever wish we had our own children?" asked Helen.

"For the longest while, I wanted my own children. Elizabeth and I tried and tried. But, I just think it wasn't meant to be. I feel like I'm here to care for the children without fathers – Molly, the boys, all the kids at the orphanage. They're the best family I could have ever hoped for," said Jacob.

Helen smiled. "It's a shame I didn't have any girls," said Helen. "I sometimes feel like Molly must feel a little out of place amongst all of those boys".

"She seems perfectly content to me," said Jacob.

"Besides, she's always lost in a book or trying out for some play or another. I don't think she feels like she's missing out on anything," said Jacob.

"She'll soon be a grown woman, Jacob. Are you ready for all of that?" said Helen.

"Why, that's why I have my shotgun," said Jacob chuckling.

"I think she'll choose well. After all, she had you as a role model," said Helen giving him a soft kiss.

"Maybe we should go check on the children," said Jacob. "I haven't heard their voices in a while."

Helen agreed and they walked down to the shore. They found the fishing poles, but no children. Jacob called out for them. Helen called out for them. There was no reply. Indeed, no one seemed to be around at all.

"Maybe they went for a walk," said Helen.

They tried not to worry about it and went back to set up lunch. After an hour had passed, Helen began to get anxious.

"I'll go search for them in the woods," said Jacob. He walked off into the dense forest along a trail he found. About a mile in, he could no longer tell in which direction the path led.

"Molly, William," he yelled at the top of his lungs.

In a few hours it would be dark, Jacob ran to the left looking for any sign of them. He began to feel afraid that he would get lost in the forest. He found his way back to the trail. When he walked out of the trees, Helen was waiting for him. When she saw he was alone, she started to cry. It was getting dark and she was frantic. The air was getting colder. They could no longer see to search for them.

"What if there are bears? Are there bears in England?" cried Helen.

Jacob soothed his wife assuring her that the children had simply wandered in the wrong direction and they would find them in the morning. Helen refused to leave. They didn't have a tent, so Jacob made a makeshift shelter out of blankets and tree branches. He made an extra-large fire hoping the children would maybe be able to see it from far off. Helen's mind filled with fear and worst case scenarios. Jacob found some bourbon in the carriage and tried to get her to drink some to calm her nerves. After a few hours of sobbing, she fell asleep shivering in his arms.

As soon as the sun came up, Jacob and Helen were on their feet. They knew they couldn't cover a lot of ground with just the two of them. So, Jacob took the carriage to a nearby farmhouse to ask for assistance. An old man named Zachary and his son Fleming offered to return with him and help search for the little ones. So, they set off in pairs. Jacob and Helen searched one direction and Zachary and Fleming took the other. Jacob called out names until his voice was hoarse and then Helen started calling.

Finally, they heard what sounded like a whimpering sound coming from the bottom of the ravine. Helen and Jacob scrambled down the hill, slipping on the dirt and rocks as they made their way down the steep embankment. They found the children in a pile at the bottom. The three youngest were at the bottom of the pile. William was near the top and appeared to be the one crying. Upon closer inspection, they noticed his leg was broken. On top of all of them was Molly encircling them with her body in an attempt to keep the younger ones warm. Her fingers were covered in frostbite and she was cold to the touch. At first she wasn't responsive when they tried to shake her.

"Molly, Molly wake up," said Jacob.

He picked her up off of the pile of boys. Helen tended to William, wrapping his leg in a handkerchief that she found in Jacob's pocket. The three younger boys seemed tired and hungry, but relatively unharmed aside from some scratches and bruises. Jacob wrapped Molly in his coat and rubbed her cheeks. She opened her eyes.

"We have to get them to a doctor," said Helen.

"Can you carry Molly?" Jacob asked.

Helen said, "Yes, I think I can."

Jacob handed her to Helen and picked up William. They asked the little ones to follow them up the hill. It was a slow process and Molly was a bit too heavy for Helen, so they had to take frequent breaks. At long last, they made it back to their carriage where Zachary and Fleming were waiting for them, relieved that the whole party had been found. Zachary suggested going back to his place in his carriage and Fleming would take Jacob's carriage to fetch a doctor.

When they arrived at Zachary's farm, his wife, Edna came out and greeted them. She boiled a pot of hot water and set Molly down on the sofa, wrapping her in blankets. William was laid on a bed where Helen tried to soothe him in his pain. Once she could see the injured were stable, Edna went into the kitchen to make some food for the little ones. After about twenty minutes, the color started to return to Molly's cheeks.

"Papa, is that you?" she asked.

"I'm here," said Jacob. "What happened?"

Molly became more alert and started to explain, "I had been reading Peter Pan. So, I pretended that I was Wendy and was taking the boys to Neverland. I set off into the woods telling them we were going on a grand adventure. But, then William tripped and fell down a ravine. I went after him with the boys, but his leg was broken and I couldn't carry him. So, I told the boys to stay with him, while I went for help. But, I couldn't find the way back. I came back and tried to keep them warm. I'm sorry, Papa. I know I let you down," said Molly.

"You and your fanciful ideas in those books. Life isn't a fictional story, Molly. You're lucky to be alive," Jacob said crossly.

Then realizing he was really just angry to have almost lost her, he softened his tone.

"The important thing is that you're alright. I don't know what I would do without you," said Jacob. "Rest, the doctor will be here soon".

The doctor arrived within the hour and tended to William first. He was in a great deal of pain and cried out when the doctor set his leg. The doctor gave him some morphine and told Helen and Jacob he needed to stay off the leg for a while. He said he would bring out a pair of crutches later that the boy could use.

Molly was in a bit worse condition than they had thought. Two of her toes were completely black and the doctor had to amputate them. He credited her quick thinking to encircle the other boys with saving their lives.

"It can be quite cold at night in England this time of year. You could have found them all dead. She'll be in pain for a while, but she'll be alright. Just keep her tightly bundled tonight," said Dr. Cornish.

Helen and Jacob thanked the doctor. Zachary insisted the family stay the night until the family was in better shape. Molly asked about the others and started to eat some soup. William faded in and out of consciousness from the morphine, but by nightfall was able to eat some supper. The three younger boys seemed bored and restless and wanted to go home.

The next morning, they helped Molly and William into the carriage and went back to the hotel. They were supposed to leave on the ship back to America in the morning, but Jacob was unsure they were ready for travel. He went and exchanged the tickets for a week later. Henry came by to see Jacob and was shocked by the tale of their family picnic gone awry. He offered to help in any way he could. Jacob sent him to get some groceries and declined further offers to go out on the town in London. The family spent the next week in isolation, helping the children regain their strength for the long voyage.

One night, after the children had fallen asleep, Helen brought up the subject of Molly.

"I believe that one is going to be a handful as a teenager, Jacob. She has such an imagination, leading those boys off into the woods like that. I'm grateful she has a compassionate heart and kept them warm, but think of what could have happened. I worry for her and what trouble she might get herself into. I had romantic notions in my head too once and that's how I was charmed by Wayne. I hope that girl has more sense than I had," said Helen.

That night Jacob tossed and turned thinking about the truth in what Helen had said. He wondered if perhaps he had given her too much freedom and vowed to keep a closer eye on her. He couldn't let anything happen to her. He was, after all, as the Grandmaster had said, the protector of the light.

25

When Anna arrived home, she called out for Midge excitedly. She hadn't answered the door and wasn't in the living room or kitchen. She found Midge ironing her work uniform in the guest room. Midge looked up and smiled at Anna who was beaming and looked beautiful in her light green blouse with her round belly. Her hair was pulled back in a ponytail. She wore a shimmery coral lipstick and seemed to glow.

"Well, there you are, pudding cake. I was worried about you driving all that way with a bun in the oven. I've started packing up some of your things and ironed your nice dress clothes for your new job," said Midge.

"Oh Midge, you're the best. I'm really going to miss you in North Carolina," said Anna.

"I'll miss you too, sugar, but you don't pay old Midge no mind. You just send me pictures of that baby on the Facebook, you hear?" said Midge hugging Anna.

Midge unplugged the iron and sat on the bed.

"Now you told me the short version on the phone, but I want to hear all the details now that you're here," said Midge.

Anna told her all about the new job, Ben's house and

their romantic time together.

"Are you sure about moving in together, darling, you haven't known that boy too long. I'm just looking out for ya," said Midge.

"I know. I worried about that too. But, everything just feels so right. His home feels like my home. I can sit on the deck overlooking the ocean and write. It's perfect," said Anna.

"Well, from the looks of ya, the boy seems to have put the vim back in your vigor. Anything goes wrong you know who to call," said Midge. "What are your plans while you're in town? I've got the boys on standby to get the U-Haul ready".

"Oh, I think I'd like to take a couple of days to just visit all the old places. I thought I should drop by my mom's and talk to my sister. I wanted to finish up this writing project I've been working on, pack, that sort of thing. I was hoping I could maybe get one last meal of your turkey pot pie," said Anna with a wink.

"That baby sure does like that turkey pot pie. We'll have it tonight. Get yourself comfortable. That's a long drive for a pregnant woman. I'll get to cooking," said Midge.

Anna stared at the packed boxes and set her suitcase down next to them. She had lived in this place her entire life. It would be strange living somewhere new. She told Midge she was going out for a while and drove up and down side streets, memories flooding her mind. She passed the dance club from the night Callie was conceived, looking desolate and somewhat out of place in the afternoon light. She stopped by the library, drove past the theater where Patrick worked.

She finally stopped by the bookstore and made her way to the comfy armchair that she considered "her spot." She wondered if she would have a new coffeehouse to go to, where she would hang out, what her life would be like in North Carolina. She was excited about the job. Oddly, home seemed foreign to her now that she had been with Ben. She missed him and couldn't wait to get back.

She pulled out Jacob's diary from her backpack, prepared to read the last few pages and finish the draft before dinner. She had never identified with Molly while reading it, Molly always seemed so much more noble than Anna. But, the story about Molly leading the boys off into the woods on a Peter Pan quest seemed exactly like something she would do. She smiled and wondered how it would end. Her cellphone rang. It was Ben.

"Did you make it back safely?" Ben asked.

"Oh yeah, I'm sorry I meant to call. I was talking to Midge and got sidetracked. I miss you. I can't wait until I get home," said Anna.

"I love to hear you call it home," said Ben.

"I know. Crazy isn't it?" said Anna.

"Crazy good," said Ben.

"I'll call you before I leave to drive down there," said Anna.

"I love you," said Ben.

"I love you, too," said Anna.

She got up to order a caramel macchiato from the coffee kiosk in the bookstore, blew on the hot foam and sat for a few minutes before continuing with her reading.
By the time she finished reading, she barely had time to type. The words flew from her fingertips. The story was finally coming together. She hoped that Jacob would be pleased with the draft. It had turned out somewhat different than she initially thought, but she could see now why Jacob wanted the story told. As she typed the final words and hit save, she realized it was almost time for dinner and she needed to get home to Midge. She browsed for a minute through the bookstore and found *A Locals Guide to North Carolina*, which she paid for at the counter before leaving.

Midge was pulling the steaming hot pot pie out of the oven when she returned.

"I thought I was going to have to call you. You have to eat turkey pot pie right out of the oven while the crust is still crispy," said Midge.

"I know. I'm sorry I'm late. I went to the bookstore and you know how I can lose track of time in a bookstore," said Anna.

"Well, set the table and get to eating. I bet that baby's hungry," said Midge.

Just then, the baby gave Anna a swift kick in the belly as if to agree with Midge.

"I think you're right Midge – as always," said Anna.

The two ate dinner together and then spent the evening on the couch watching *The Golden Girls*. Midge laughed heartily wrapped in a blanket on her favorite chair with her feet propped up on an ottoman. Anna sprawled across the couch eating chocolate and smiling. She was happy to finally be finished with the book and couldn't wait to visit Jacob in the morning. She looked over and Midge was asleep in her chair, her mouth open and loudly snoring.

Anna got up and walked over to pull the blanket up to her chin. Midge had been really good to her. She hated to leave her there all alone. Anna walked into the kitchen and baked some cinnamon rolls for the morning to surprise Midge. She paced about the house, unable to sleep. She would try to lie down, but she was beginning to feel uncomfortable and the baby kept kicking her in the side.

She wondered what Patrick was up to and popped open her laptop to check Facebook. *Well, look there, he was in a relationship.* At least it was the same girl she had caught him with. *Well, all's well that ends well*, Anna thought. He looked happy. She let go of her petty jealousy and felt glad for a moment that everyone had found some happiness.

"Goodbye Patrick. Fare thee well," she said and clicked out of Facebook.

She yawned and pulled up her manuscript to read

through it. She wondered if someone would publish it. She hooked up the printer and watched as hundreds of pages fed through the machine. She couldn't believe she actually completed a project so large. She put a rubber band around the pages and slipped them into her backpack for tomorrow. She leaned over and looked at the clock – 2:00 a.m. *Time for sleep, baby*, she said to herself, rubbing her stomach. After a few minutes, she finally drifted off.

The next morning she drove out to the cemetery. It had been nearly a year since she had first encountered Jacob. So much had happened in a year. She almost couldn't believe it. Once again, she was guided by instinct to the sawhorse markers and parked the car. She pulled the manuscript out of her backpack and made her way down the hill. As the statue came into view, she was struck by the fact that it was a female statue. This was Jacob Hoffner's grave and yet, it wasn't marked by a man on a horse or some type of phallic shaped Washington monument type marker. It was marked by the statue of a beautiful woman.

Anna thought of all of the female influences on Jacob's life, his wife Elizabeth, his second wife Helen and his adopted daughter, Molly. Here was a man who in the 1800s really respected women and held them in the highest esteem. She smiled and touched the marble statue examining its features, its beautiful hair and strong arms. She walked over to the steps and sat down waiting. The wind was cool and quiet. It struck her that she no longer felt the need to escape the world coming here. But, that coming here somehow enlarged her world. How would she make it in a new place without this presence, this guidance to light her way? She closed her eyes and prayed to have this feeling follow her wherever she went.

When she opened them, Jacob was standing there, leaning against one of the lion statues. She held up the manuscript as if to show him and he smiled.

"I see you finished," he said.

"I did," said Anna. "You did so much for this community. You started the orphanage and built up the school system. The citizens of Northside should really know what a great contribution you made. I was happy I could write it all down for you. There's just one thing I don't understand".

"Oh, what's that?" asked Jacob.

"It's a beautiful story," said Anna.

"You did a beautiful job writing it," said Jacob.

"But, it's not really about you," said Anna with some hesitation. "I mean, it is, but it isn't".

"No, who's it about?" said Jacob.

"Well, in the end it seemed like it was really about Molly," said Anna.

"That's where you're wrong, my dear," said Jacob.

Anna looked confused.

"The story is about Molly, but it's really about you," said Jacob.

"Me? How is the story about me?" asked Anna.

"Because you are Molly's great grand-daughter and you, my child, are her legacy," said Jacob.

26

As Molly grew, Jacob was ever watchful of her suitors. She maintained her love of books, but became increasingly interested in helping Helen out at the orphanage. Sister Catherine was getting up in years and could hardly perform her duties. So, Molly took over much of the care of the children. Molly spent long hours at the orphanage, often going there right after school and not returning until after midnight. Jacob was fine with this arrangement as long as she kept up her studies.

She didn't date at all until after she graduated and even then, very little. She seemed passionately concerned about the welfare of others and gave little thought to herself. Helen often fretted that she feared Molly might become something of a spinster, but Jacob was happy to have her still at home and in their company.

News of unrest in the South spread and there was talk of civil war. Jacob, much too old to go off to battle, feared for the fate of Helen's boys. William had been a great help at Hoffner & Clark and had talked of taking over the business after Jacob was gone. His leg had healed somewhat improperly and he had a limp. So, when the war broke out, he was asked to stay behind and run the business with Jacob while the three younger boys were sent off to the front.

Long a supporter of abolitionist causes, Molly became restless and wanted to assist in the war effort. Jacob discovered she had secretly been taking nursing classes at the local hospital. She had become more and more strong-willed as she got older and one day simply announced that she was going to be a nurse in the war and there was nothing to be done about it.

"I have to go, Papa. I have the proper training. I can be of great help," Molly pleaded.

"Your place is here. They need you at the orphanage. Helen may lose all of her boys except William. I cannot lose you," said Jacob.

"The sister can manage the orphanage just fine. They need people with medical training. Hundreds of men are dying every day with no one beside them to help them. You've always been very good to me, Papa. But, I'm sorry I'm going whether you like it or not," said Molly.

She gathered her things and left out the door. Jacob spoke not another word to her.

As he lay awake at night in bed wondering what had happened to her, he was sorry they had parted on such bad terms. He wished he had hugged her and told her he had loved her before she went. He remembered the glowing light that surrounded her at Stonehenge and thought of those dying men seeing that light before they died. He thought of how she had sacrificed herself in the woods for her brothers. In that moment, he realized that this work was Molly's destiny. He just prayed she would return home alive.

Molly saved hundreds of men in the War and bore witness to the deaths of hundreds of others. She promised to write notes to girlfriends and wives. She sang lullabies and rubbed the foreheads of boys no older than 16. It was heartbreaking, tough work but Molly cared for each young man as if he was her own brother.

At home, Helen wailed as she received reports that all of her boys had died in battle. She sewed quilts and sent rations to the troops. Jacob tried to comfort her, but she leaned on William, not wanting to burden her husband. She remembered how ashamed she was when Jacob saw her after her beatings by Wayne and she hated for him to see her weakened once more. William married and bore her a grandson whom she doted on and loved to hold, remembering her lost boys and how she had cared for them as infants.

When the war ended, Molly returned home, nearly 30 and looking much older than her years. She spent her days working at the orphanage and her nights working at the local hospital. Jacob apologized to her for how they had left things.

"It's O.K. Papa, I understand," she said and smiled bearing no grudge toward the old man.

He began to think her light had dimmed; she was so haggard and tired from endless work. She continued to live in the house, sometimes stopping by to see William and his new family.

One afternoon, when she was nearing 40 and Jacob was a very old man, she returned from work with a smile on her face and a skip in her step.

"I've met someone, Papa – a doctor at the hospital. His name is Frederick and he's incredibly kind. He's asked me to marry him," she said.

Helen and Jacob were overwhelmed by the news, not expecting Molly to ever marry and were overjoyed by her happiness. Molly and her new husband acquired a small farmhouse on the outskirts of town and within months, Molly was pregnant.

But, as the time drew near for the birth, tragedy struck Molly once more. Her husband, Frederick, had contracted cholera from a patient at the hospital and died two days before the birth. Molly held her son in her arms and swore she would raise him as a kind man, a man his father would have been proud of. She tried to smile at the funeral, not wanting the baby's first memories to be of pain and heartache. Jacob wiped her tears from her eyes with his handkerchief at the funeral and promised her everything would be alright.

Jacob offered to have Molly and the boy, whom she named Samuel, move back in to the house with Helen and himself. But, she wanted to do things on her own. She hired some help to tend the cows on her land and continued to work at the hospital. Samuel was the light of her life and she lit up every time he came near her. She brought him over to visit Jacob. The boy enjoyed playing with his cousin, Peter, William's boy.

Helen passed in April of that year and Jacob buried her in the ancestral plot not far from his Elizabeth. Molly helped him with the arrangements. He would come by and visit Samuel and bring her flowers from the gardens. She would check in on him and bring him a pot of soup or a loaf of bread and make sure he was taking care of himself.

It was a simple life, but a good one. Years passed and Jacob enjoyed the company of his family and friends. As Jacob neared the century mark, he became more frail and needed help to get around. His immune system was no longer what it used to be and when William's son, Peter contracted pneumonia, Jacob was struck down too. The boy, being young and strong, recovered quickly. But, Jacob was bedridden for months. It became obvious to everyone that he didn't have much longer. As Jacob was overcome with fever and ready to pass from this world, Molly sat by his side day and night rubbing cold rags on his hot forehead. He noticed that she was glowing, shining brightly at his side, and he no longer feared the end, for he knew when the moment came and his darkness descended, that her light would shine on.

27

"Molly was my great grandmother?" said Anna incredulously.

"Yes," said Jacob. "She was."

Anna struggled to grasp what he was saying.

"But, I thought you wanted me to write down your life story, so people would know your great works and that I could fulfill my dream of writing a novel. That's what you said, right?" said Anna.

She felt like she had somehow been misled.

"What was my job as Grandmaster in regard to Molly?" Jacob asked.

"You were the protector of the light," said Anna.

"That's right," said Jacob. "And that is why I am sitting here talking to you instead of Molly herself. For you see, Molly is the light. She is quite literally an angel in heaven and it is your job, Anna to continue her legacy."

"But, I don't understand," said Anna. "I'm nothing like her. Have you heard nothing I've told you? She was self-sacrificing and giving. She lived her whole life helping other people. A year ago, I was working in a warehouse, involved in a messed up relationship and doing nothing with my life," Anna protested.

"And now?" Jacob asked.

"Now, I have a job writing for a children's home, a house by the ocean with a man I love and a baby on the way," said Anna.

"And you've written a book," said Jacob.

"O.K. true. I'm in a better place than I was a year ago, but that doesn't exactly make me an angel," said Anna.

"Molly was always guided by her light. She could see her light and others could see it emanating from her. It emanates from you too, although you cannot see it. Molly's gift was caring for others. It was her purpose on this planet. My purpose was to protect her light. Your purpose is to write. It is your gift in this world," said Jacob.

Anna absorbed what the ghost was saying and began to feel lighter.

"So you came to me to show me the light?" asked Anna.

"Indeed," said Jacob. "I saw you come here, month after month, glowing just like my Molly but with no perception of it. I saw your pain and your struggle and I wanted to help you. You see even though I am no longer of this world, I still think of myself as a protector of the light. I had you write the novel, partly so the world could know of what Molly and I did on this earth. But, I also did it for you. I thought by using your gift, by writing the words, you might finally be able to see your light and be guided by it," said Jacob.

"I do," said Anna. "I consider this story such a blessing," she said clutching the manuscript in her hands. "I'll make sure it gets published. I'm so very proud of my great grandmother, and you. Thank you," said Anna.

"You're welcome. I'm glad you can see it now and you can show it to your daughter. It is always there, guiding you, you just have to believe in it," said Jacob.

"Will I ever see you again?" asked Anna.

"I will always be with you, you will feel me in the

ocean breeze and see me in the glimmer of your daughter's eyes," said Jacob. And with that, the old man faded from view and was gone.

Anna blinked and was once again aware of the solitude of the place. She stared out over the headstones and felt a profound sense of peace. She felt stronger, more confident than she ever had before, like her life was worth something, it had meaning and she had a purpose for living.

She stood up, smoothed her sweatshirt over her burgeoning belly. She walked slowly to the car realizing this is the last time she would visit this place. She turned and looked back, trying to engrave the memory of it into her mind, but knowing she would never forget what had happened here.

When she returned home, Midge questioned her knowing smile. Anna simply said she was happy and asked Midge to arrange for the movers in the morning. She spent the rest of the day packing, having her medical records moved and shutting down bank accounts. She called her mother, told her all about her new job, the baby and Ben. Anna's mother was used to hearing news from her daughter last minute. But, she was surprised to hear Anna say that she loved her before she hung up. Anna held the phone surprised that she had invited her mother out to see her new place on the beach. Maybe it was time for a new beginning for them too.

As Anna rolled up her sleeves and put the last of the boxes into the U-Haul, she gave Midge the longest hug.

"You come out and visit me on the beach, Midge. Make that Brad give you some days off. I'll put you up in the guest room. We'll watch *Golden Girls* and collect seashells on the beach. It will be great," said Anna.

"Sure thing, pudding cake," said Midge.

Anna drove east toward her new home, boxes rattling in the backseat, a box of chocolate raisins in her passenger seat next to her cell phone signaling the GPS. She sang along to the radio and happily munched the chocolate. She took several bathroom breaks along the way, her worries about the past fading with each mile. As she edged closer to the beach, she rolled down her windows to smell the salty air.

It smelled like home.

28

As Anna rocked her new baby daughter on the back deck, she stared out at the immensity of the ocean and was filled with gratitude. Ben was out showing a house. He had fixed her eggs and fruit that morning before leaving and had warmed the baby's bottle and fed her while Anna slept.

Anna was doing a little bit of work from home. She planned to write some press releases while the baby took her afternoon nap.

The months prior had been filled with the excitement of her new job. She had met all of the children at the home and wanted to take home each of their adoring faces. She had tirelessly worked on writing a grant for a new playground and got the funding. Shortly before she went on maternity leave, they installed it. It was such a blessing to see their smiling faces climb the jungle gym and swing on the swings that she had acquired for them through her writing. She loved her job. She never felt tired and always wanted to write more, do whatever she could to make sure those children had the best life possible.

Living with Ben was an easy adjustment. They just seemed to easily fit into each other's worlds. They gave each other the perfect balance of togetherness and alone time. He had rubbed her feet every night of her pregnancy, gone out for midnight ice cream runs and held her hand through the labor pains. His job allowed him to be home a lot so they had enjoyed getting to know each other these past two months that she had stayed home with the baby. They just fit together. The relationship felt almost effortless. She never worried where it was headed or what he was doing. They just felt like they belonged together.

Anna looked down at the resting infant in her arms with the little brown curls on her forehead. "Callie Angelina" they had called her – a beautiful angel descended from a beautiful angel. Anna looked up at the sky and thought about Molly and what Molly might have thought of this beautiful little cherub.

Anna's mother had been for a visit the week before along with her sister. For some reason, the rift between them felt like it had been sealed. Her mother was overjoyed at having a granddaughter and her sister seemed tickled about being an aunt. Anna thought perhaps her prior judgment of them had been more about her own inadequate feelings than any real dislike of her on their part. She called more often and felt like, at long last, she was part of a real and loving family.

Ben had introduced her to his friends on the beach. There was Carol, the interior designer and her husband, Derek. They were funny and loved being competitive at their game night parties. She had also met Tricia, who she worked with at the children's home and her husband, John. They were more serious types, but Tricia had been a great help to Anna. She brought over food right after she had the baby and had offered to babysit. Anna felt like she really fit in and was part of the community.

Anna had sent the novel to a publisher, but hadn't heard back yet. She was determined to keep sending it until someone agreed to put it in print. She couldn't wait to hold it in her hand. She imagined her daughter reading it and how she would explain to Callie the story of it all and how she fit into the legacy of her ancestors.

She held the infant closer, smelling her hair and rocking her. Callie opened her eyes, looking around, alert.

"Well, good morning, Beautiful," Anna said. The baby cooed and smiled back at her.

"Shall we go check the mail?" she said to the baby and rested the baby's head on her shoulder so she could stand up.

She walked through the patio doors, through the living room and gently opened the front door with one hand. She wrapped the blanket around the baby to protect her from the breeze and made her way barefoot down the salty stairs to the sidewalk and sang as she walked to the mailbox. She pulled open the handle and felt around. Her fingers caught the edge of an envelope, which she grabbed and tucked under her arm to take back into the house.

She set the baby down in her playard to crawl around and sat down on the nearby armchair to open the letter. It was from Simon & Schuster. She tore open the envelope.

"Dear Ms. Perrault, we are happy to inform you that we have chosen to publish your novel, *Legacy*," it said.

The rest of the words became a blur. She was so excited she wanted to scream.

"Oh my God, baby girl," she exclaimed in an animated voice. "They're going to publish it!" she squealed. The baby just looked at her and smiled. Anna jumped up and down doing a happy dance.

Ben walked in an hour later and Anna still couldn't wipe the grin off her face. She told him the news and he grabbed her, so excited for her. He offered to take the baby while she called everyone to tell them the good news. She spent the rest of the day tending to the baby and watching TV with Ben. She finished her press releases and called to let Tricia know. Ben made her a special dinner and afterwards they had key lime pie out on the back deck and watched the sun disappear on the horizon. It was a simple life, but a good one. She went to sleep that night, feeling the light within her growing. It was so strong; it seemed to encompass her while she slept. She could feel the glow of it surround her. It was so warm and comforting.

She woke early in the morning and went to check on Callie in her crib. She kissed her softly on the head and tiptoed out of the room. She stopped by their bedroom and kissed Ben on the head and told him it was almost time to get up. Anna made her way into the kitchen and started the coffee maker. She pulled one of Ben's mugs out of the cabinet, poured herself a cup of coffee and sat down. She opened the newspaper and spooned sugar into the steaming brew.

As she poured the cream into the cup, she held up the mug to look at it. It was one of Ben's Thoreau mugs. She smiled as she read it, "When one advances confidently in the direction of one's dreams and endeavors to live the life which he has imagined, he will meet with a success unexpected in common hours." *Yes*, Anna thought to herself, *you just have to believe and follow the light*.

53349054R00116

Made in the USA
Lexington, KY
30 June 2016